DREAMSINGER

DREAMSINGER

The Whale Who Would Save The World!

Screenplay by
Tony White

Inspired by the book "The Prince of Whales" by R. L. Fisher

~ and with script assistance by Bob Silverstein

First Printing 2019

ISBN: 978-0-9964279-8-2

A **DRAWASSIC** book

www.drawastic.com

"FILMS I NEVER GOT TO MAKE":

Why did DRAWASSIC decide to publish a series of animated movie scripts that I have never made? Simple because, having struggled for a lifetime to get support for my filmmaking visions and meeting nothing but apathy and disinterest from the industry, I at least wanted to the public to have a chance to see what I say, to share a vision of animated filmmaking that is different to the mainstream and yet – I believe – has a valid voice in the world of entertainment filmmaking. The scripts published in this series are not all written by me but are certainly molded by what I was trying to achieve with animation – and they are certainly very different in style and approach. Once upon a time, when a certain Walt Disney has a unique vision and animation was pushed further and further towards imaginative storytelling and groundbreaking visual originality there was a chance to go beyond the formulaic and the predictable. Now all that has changed of course and despite my having made over 200 TV commercials (many award-winning), two TV Specials, several Short Films (one of which winning a BAFTA) and the title sequence for "The Pink Panther Strikes Again" movie, I have never been given a chance to show what I can do with a full-length movie venture – either in the mainstream or indie worlds. It is not as if my ideas were to out there and strange for modern audiences. Indeed, I challenge readers to deny that when reading the scripts I am publishing in this series of books. It's more the fact that the industry today has preconceived ideas of what audiences what, applying formulas of design, storytelling and subject matter that the industry, in its infinite wisdom, deems worthy of laying before modern audiences. It doesn't help too that with the advent of technology and the digital revolution the old-school notion of hand-drawn animation is no longer fashionable, unless of course is can be compromised and fashioned into what is deemed formulaic enough for the industry norms. I hope therefore in publishing these scripts readers will be able to make their own minds up on what is appealing to animation audiences and what is not. Remember however that all of these scripts are *"first-draft"* screenplays and have yet to go through the production mill that will enable many minds and many artistic

talents to form them into what might be an amazing animated experience. Nevertheless, I feel confident that the subject matter of each script will speak for itself and hint at what might have been, were there a little more vision, imagination and creative bravery in the industry they were designed for.

I thank you for giving this script a fair hearing in the court of public opinion!

Sincerely,

Tony White.

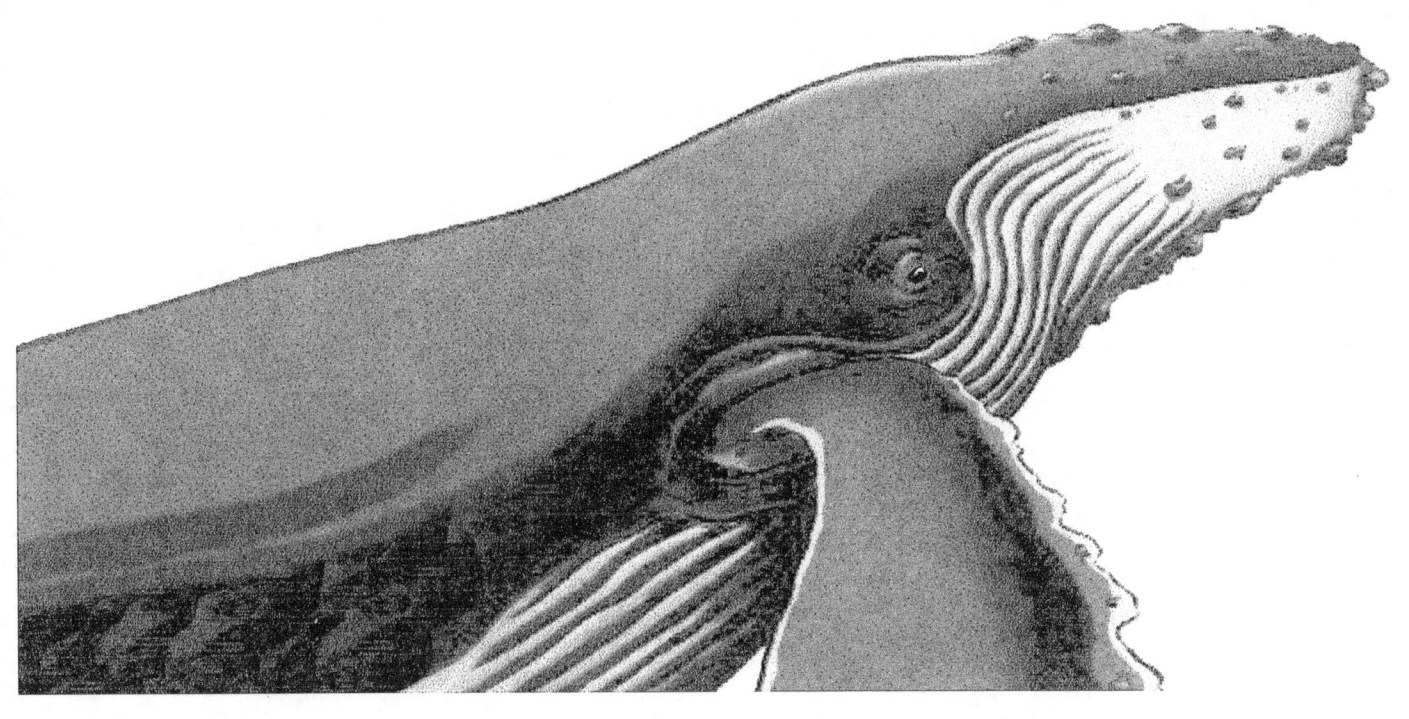

Beautiful whale concept art created in 1992 by **Alan Kerswell**

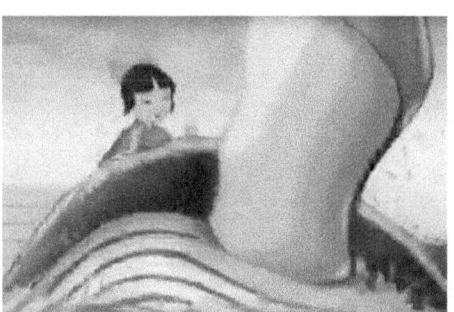
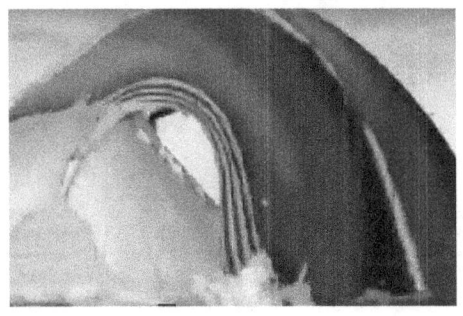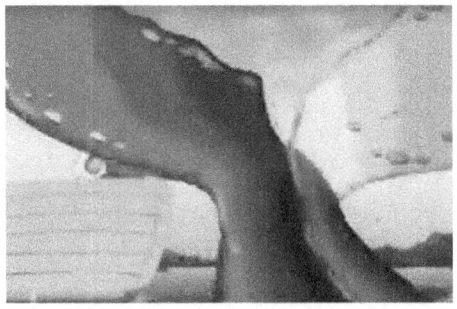

A test animation sequence of *"Mitsu"* and *"Toby"*. This was created in 1992, using traditional hand-drawn animation and CG rendered layers, somewhat similar to the techniques used in *"Who Framed Roger Rabbit"* in 1988. Working with **Effi Wizen** at **Bibo TV** in Germany at the time, we were pushing the limits of where the technology could take us in those days. It was important to us that although we respected the kind of artistic sensibilities that Hayao Miyazaki was creating with a drawn Japanese style in his animation, we were also looking to establish a 3D style of animated rendering for the creatures beneath the ocean that somehow contrasted with it in a compatible way.

A great number of raindrops have fallen into the ocean over the last few decades that have unfolded since I first wrote this screenplay. It all began when a very dear friend and literary agent contact of mine, Bob Silverstein, gave me a book – "The Prince of Whales" by R. L. Fisher – and said I should read it with both my animation and spiritual hats on. I had been visiting him in New York State at the time, following a business trip relating to an animated advertising project. I was about to board a plane to return to my native London and he said he thought it would be good reading for the flight. I don't normally like to read books on planes. However on this occasion I found "The Prince of Whales" impossible to put down. The book was fun to read but somehow, deep inside, it touched on issues that that really hit deep. The first thing I did when I got back to my London-based studio at the time was to call Bob to negotiate a film option with him for the story. I thought that with a little work and a little modification it had the potential of being an animated classic for the age we were living in.

Getting an option on the book for a year or two, I proceeded to write the script. The book was set around a community of whales and treated them in quite an anthropomorphic way. However, I wanted to create something deeper that presented the whale community in its own right, on its own terms and seen entirely from their perspective. Although my final screenplay still has quite an anthropomorphic quality to it, I really struggled to try and have the whales speak from themselves. In all honesty I failed totally with my first draft. I spent something like two intensive months drafting out something, working day and night. Then as I tend to do, I put the manuscript in a drawer for a couple of weeks and didn't touch it. I wanted to put a little distance between the writing and the objective reading I was about to do. However, much to my frustration, when I did eventually bring myself to read it I became immediately disappointed by the fact that it just didn't read as I wanted it to read. I went to bed that night feeling especially low, in view of all of the blood, sweat and tears I'd put into it previously. Then the most amazing thing happened. That night I actually dreamed the entire story as it is written now! I woke up at something like 3:00am with the whole thing running through my head again and again, so I simply had to get up and type it out. The whole unbroken process took something like 12 hours. In the process it became the story that I'd always hoped to write in the first place!

I personally believe my director's vision for the film was quite groundbreaking at the time. This all happened in the reasonably early days of 3D animation, and

although I am a passionate diehard for traditional 2D animation – a "luddite" some might say – I saw an argument for this film being created using both 2D and 3D animation. As you'll soon see, the story works in two worlds – the world beneath the waves and the world above the waves. I consequently wanted to capture the true underwater, three-dimensional, almost foggy-focused sensation that being submerged offered. Yet I didn't want a "cartoon" style for this, so I approached an amazing artist friend – Michael Emden – who created the beautiful concept art that decorates the cover of this book. This was very close to the look I wanted for the underwater sequences in the movie. As you'll also see when you read the screenplay, the world above the water storyline is set in Japan. So I wanted to venture towards a style of 2D animation for that which was somewhere between the traditional Japanese "Ukiyo-e" print style and the more mature approaches associated with the anime tradition – more specifically, those by the great Japanese director, Hayao Miyazaki. This combination of animation approaches alone would have made this film a groundbreaking animated concept at the time that had not been done before.

The story has a very strong environmental theme to it, set against the backdrop of the whaling industry. Even all those decades ago I felt passionately that whale hunting should cease and that we, as a species, needed to educate ourselves on the destruction we were inflicting on our planet and our environment. I therefore saw this story as something that would reach out to the current and future generations and perhaps have an effect on the increasing damage we were doing. Sadly, as I write this in 2019, we have seemingly learned nothing whatsoever - and as a result our planet, and the whales in its oceans. are under more threat than ever before! I consequently feel that this film has as much relevance now – if not significantly more – than it had when I first read "The Prince of Whales" book! This reality is a source of great regret to me, of course, as I would much rather that there would no longer be a need for this film, and we humans have cleaned up our act, and our planet, significantly. But alas, it is not so.

The biggest struggles I have had in getting this film off the ground have been in dealing with Hollywood. I have not found the least bit of interest from the mainstream industry whatsoever. Indeed, I have instead received a significant amount of rejection, dismissal and even hostility. For example, as you will read, the lead human character in the story is a young Japanese girl, Mitsu. The notion of having a young Japanese lead received a lot of kickbacks whenever I presented it. I was told that no one in America would ever pay to see an animated movie with a significant girl character, especially a significant Japanese girl character!

In addition, because didn't conform to the traditional, musical, Disney princess kind of stereotypical approach, there was much resistance. Dealing with whales and their pursuit by humans seemed to make the film both "political" and "violent" in many people's eyes. Indeed, one producer told me that she had a 6-year-old daughter and there was no way on earth that she would allow her daughter to see such a "violent" and "traumatizing" animated movie. I was truly shocked by this remark and asked why she felt that, as in my mind it was in no way either of those things. She replied that she particularly objected to the fact that (trying to avoid story spoilers here!) a significant character was "killed off" in the film at the very beginning and this would have a terrible psychological affect on her daughter if she saw that fact. I responded that the story did not in fact do what she was claiming it was doing. I then asked her if she allowed her daughter to see "Bambi"? She said she did - in fact it was one of her daughter's favorite films. I then pointed out that "Dreamsinger" did not go anywhere nearly as far as what actually happens in Bambi. Indeed, I wondered if that particular producer had even read the script in the first place!

A second opposition I got from the industry at large was the fact that I wanted to use the groundbreaking 2D and 3D animation approach I mentioned earlier. Several influential people told me that this would not be possible, as it just would not work - although I still do not know what they were seeing in their heads compared to what I was seeing in mind. Many also confirmed to me that having a Japanese girl lead could never work with American audiences. I can confirm however that a couple of years later that not only did Pixar take the hugely successful "Finding Nemo" movie to the kind of underworld environment that I wanted for "Dreamsinger," but also Hayao Miyazaki picked up an Oscar for his 2D animated classic, "Spirited Away" – which did, incidentally, feature a young Japanese girl lead!

A third frustration I had with Hollywood was a purely on a financial level. Indeed, this one really blew me away! At one particular point on my journey I produced a budget that was shortly after the movie "Who Framed Roger Rabbit" successfully came out. The industry was terribly excited by the rebirth of classic animated characters for that film, most of which was produced in London with British talent under the leadership of triple Oscar-winner, Richard Williams. Being London based myself at the time I planned on using the very same animators for "Dreamsinger." I priced it accordingly. My budget came out to around 15m UK Pounds. (At a time when the equivalent animation budgets in Hollywood were at least three times that.) However, when I presented my budget and screenplay (which they really liked I hasten to add) another Hollywood producer actually told me that it was way too "low" and therefore they couldn't possible consider it. Their tolerance level was at least 20m dollars higher! I explained to him that I didn't need more as the budget

I had would be using the best people in London, the best production technology and even many of the team were desperate to work on it at a reduced rate due to the environmental message the film contained. Yet they still remained unmoved by such a "cheap" project in their eyes!

I would hasten to say that these are not my only reasons for subsequently avoiding Hollywood throughout my entire career, but they are the three main ones that relate to the frustrations at not getting "Dreamsinger" made.

I did of course turn to the "indie" film marketplace for funding, too. However this was equally frustrating as, although I found many producers sincerely loved the story and my vision for the film, they all told me that at that time they couldn't countenance anything above 10m dollars for the art house cinema circuits. So it seemed I was between a rock and a hard place.

Needless to say, "DREAMSINGER" is a project contains much emotional sadness for me. Yet the real pain is not so much in terms of the industry rebuffs I had to endure, but also is due to the fact in that throughout the years I've been struggling to get this very unique film off the ground, I've sadly lost several dear friends and supporters of the project – not least of all, Bob Silverstein and Michael Embden! In my wildest, starry-eyed fantasies I saw us all up on the Academy stage, picking up an Oscar for "Dreamsinger," hand in hand together! Now unfortunately, on every level, it seems that will never happen. That said, though, I am feeling at least somewhat fulfilled by the fact that I can offer you this chance to share my vision through this publication. Perhaps someone, somewhere, will one day pick it up and achieve what I could not achieve with it after I have gone, too? If so, rest assured there will be at least three of us jumping up and down "up there" - in that great animation studio above the clouds – excitedly applauding whatever accolades the film will ultimately achieve!

In the meantime, I hope you'll enjoy your reading "Dreamsinger," be touched by it, be motivated to be a better human being through it, and somehow envision in your imagination the way that I have always imagined it to look as you do so.

Swimming with the spirit…

Tony White
www.tonywhiteanimation.com

DREAMSINGER

by

TONY WHITE

"This is our hope ~ that the children born today may still have, twenty years from hence, a bit of green grass under their bare feet, a breath of clean air to breathe, a patch of blue water to sail upon, and a whale on the horizon to set them dreaming."

~ Jacques Cousteau.

PRE-TITLE SEQUENCE - SET AGAINST A BACKDROP OF STARS:

A breathtaking view of planet EARTH. We move in, closer and closer. Entering the atmosphere, we pass over azure seas, rich green forests, crystal clear lakes and show-capped mountains. We see a sparkling stretch of ocean.

> VOICE:
> At the beginning, all life was one. The creatures of the air, the creatures of the sea and the creatures of the earth all shared the same oneness of life. Each was a favored child of the 'Great Mother' - EARTH.

As we slow to a final stop the sky darkens and we see dark, oily pollution on the surface of the water.

> VOICE:
> Then one day this pervading harmony was broken. A renegade child - MAN -sought to seek advantage for himself alone, placing himself before all the other children of the Great Mother.

CUT TO ...

EXT. C/U WASTE DUMPING SHIP - NIGHT

Darkly silhouetted human figures dump a seemingly inexhaustible trail of waste containers overboard. Some sink, some add to the existing vile slick.

> VOICE:
> Man's rebellion brought a great sadness and suffering to the heart of the Great Mother. He had been the most favored of all her children but she felt betrayed.

DISSOLVE TO ....

BENEATH THE OCEAN SURFACE - SAME MOMENT.

We see the containers as they sink. Trails of black, oily poison trail behind them. They finally join an existing mountain of toxic waste. An old and derelict oil rig projects out from among it, still oozing its vile poison.

> VOICE:
> Greed and ignorance ruled Man's thinking and soon all life was polluted by his touch and the Great Mother wept. For what was once beautiful and lush and fertile now became corrupted, defiled and ugly.

The toxic waste slowly eats away at the rocky seabed beneath.

VOICE:
And as the wastes of Man etched their way deep into the
surface of the Great Mother, a dark and vengeful force
grew restless. Slowly, inexorably, a fearsome force -
DIOMEDA - began to dream of its freedom with a
ruthless and unholy delight.

The seabed suddenly shifts and creaks as it is moved by a powerful force below.

DIOMEDA
(a muffled and terrifying sound):
Grrrrrrrrrrrrrrrroooowwwwllllll!!!

The rock stretches and cracks under the pressure from below as more toxic waste
floats down.

VOICE:
But legend has it that when the Earth is in its greatest
danger a young DREAMSINGER will emerge to save it.
And so, as her silent nightmare unfolds, the Great
Mother holds her breath and prays that the legend will
at last be fulfilled.

FADE TO:

INT. ~ MITSU'S BEDROOM - NIGHT

The bedroom of a young Japanese girl, MITSU. Cool moonlight streams through the
window, flooding everything with a bluish, silvery light. The walls show a collection of
whale pictures. The door opens and her mother, MIYOKO, walks in.

MIYOKO
Come, Mitsu. Time for bed.

Miyoko closes the blinds as Mitsu climbs under the covers.

MITSU:
Oh, mother. Do I have to? You know I'll only have my
bad dreams again.

Miyoko tucks Mitsu into bed. She sits down and gently strokes her daughter's hair.

MIYOKO:
The whale dreams? They are only dreams, Mitsu. They
cannot hurt you.

MITSU:
No, but my whales get hurt!

                          MIYOKO:
          Nobody hurts whales.

                          MITSU
                    (angry):
          Father does!

Miyoko remains patient and loving.

                          MIYOKO:
          You are too hard on your father, Mitsu. He only does
          his best for us, like all good fathers.

Mitsu starts to argue but Miyoko stops her.

                          MIYOKO:
          Sssssh. Sleep, MITSU.

Mitsu snuggles down. Miyoko kisses her tenderly and switches off the bed lamp.

                          MIYOKO:
          Sweet dreams.

                          MITSU:
          I'll try!

Concerned, Miyoko gently closes the door behind her.

CUT TO:

INTERIOR - THE FAMILY LIVING ROOM

Miyoko goes to speak to her husband MASAHIRO but loses her courage. Sighing, she picks up a framed photograph.

CUT TO:

CLOSE-UP - PHOTOGRAPH IN MIYOKO'S HAND

Masahiro proudly stands next to a whaling ship's harpoon gun. The photo is old. Miyoko and Mitsu are much younger. Tosumi is a baby in his mother's arms.

CUT TO:

C/U MIYOKO'S FACE

A small tear forms in her eye.

MIYOKO:

My husband. For our daughter's sake, please, will you
not reconsider?

MASAHIRO:

No! I cannot change my job, not even for MITSU!

MIYOKO:

But her dreams!

MASAHIRO:

Enough!

Miyoko hugs the photograph close to her heart.

FADE TO BLACK

UNDERWATER - SERENITY BAY - MOONLIT NIGHT

Huge, floating, motionless humpback whale bodies, giving the impression that all the
whales are dead. We hear the distant, agonized cries of a solitary whale in torment.
But then the great, drowsy eyes open slowly. They peer around grumpily.

WHALE 1:

Not again!

WHALE 2:

Can't a whale get some sleep around here?

The source of the tormented whale sounds is revealed. It is an adolescent whale,
called TOBY. He is making terrible dream sounds as he sleeps! An old, grumpy-
looking, battle-scarred veteran whale, GRAMPUS, complains.

GRAMPUS:

Great Blue! Will you stop that infernal noise making!
You've woken the whole pod again!

The sleeping TOBY remains oblivious and continues. Toby's mother, LUMA, moves
protectively forward.

GRAMPUS:

Luma, if your son does not shut up I will...

A larger whale intervenes. It is Toby's father, BRUJON.

BRUJON:

(interrupting)
You will what, GRAMPUS?

GRAMPUS:
(blustering)
I will... I will...

BRUJON:
(threatening)
Yes?

GRAMPUS is frustrated.

GRAMPUS:
I will... call a meeting of the pod and have your son
banished! You may be our leader but this does not
permit your son to put us all at risk!

TOBY gives out another loud dream sound.

BRUJON:
And how exactly does my son put us all at risk,
Grampus?

Grampus plays to the gallery.

GRAMPUS:
(indicating Toby)
Look! Oblivious! Soon his screeching will attract the
IRON BEASTS of the earth-walkers - and we all know
what that means!

The pod flinches at the mention of Iron Beasts!

BRUJON:
There have never been Iron Beasts in this bay before.
They only prowl in the open sea when they hunt us
down.

GRAMPUS:
(angrily)
But we won't be in the bay much longer. Will we,
Brujon? Soon we'll head off on our annual pilgrimage to
the feeding grounds. What then, Brujon? Mark my
words, your son's dream sounds will bring nothing but
trouble!

TOBY wakes up and opens one drowsy eye.

TOBY:
Wha...? What's going on?

                                    LUMA:
                You've had another noisy dream, Toby.

Toby notices Grampus and the pod scowling.

                                    TOBY:
                Oooops! Did I wake everyone again?

                                    LUMA:
                Yes, you did.

                                    TOBY:
                Oh, I'm so sorry!

Grampus is unforgiving. He swims off in a huff.

FADE TO:

SERENITY BAY - SOMETIME LATER

Toby is somewhat sad and yet excited at the same time.

                                    TOBY:
                It was strange. I dreamt about a girl child - on an Iron
                Beast! She played the most beautiful song to me.

                                    BRUJON:
                Toby, there are no children on the Iron Beasts. Just men
                with harpoons and murder in their hearts. The earth-
                walkers are our enemies!

                                    TOBY
                But she wasn't like that! She was kind and - gentle!

Luma and Brujon look to each other - unbelieving.

FADE TO:

THE DARK SEA - THE OCEAN BED

An indefinable cocktail of noxious material covers the seabed. It is spreading as more
toxic material is dumped from above. The seabed suddenly shifts and groans again as
a fearsome beast beneath it, DIOMEDA, cries out for freedom.

DIOMEDA:
Growwwwwlllllll!

CUT TO:

C/U MITSU - BEDROOM AT NIGHT - SOMETIME LATER.

Miyoko sits on Mitsu's bed, cradling her crying daughter.

> MITSU:
> There was this terrible dark place at the bottom of the
> sea and... (sniff)... the earth moved and...(sniff) Oh,
> Mother, it was horrible!

> MIYOKO:
> There, there, MITSU. It was just a dream ... just a dream.

FADE TO:

BENEATH SERENITY BAY - NEXT DAY

Toby, Luma and Brujon swim peacefully together.

> TOBY:
> (enthusiastic)
> I saw the earth-walker girl in my dreams again, Father.

> BRUJON:
> Toby, you have such a vivid imagination!

> TOBY:
> But I wasn't imagining it!

> LUMA:
> (changing the subject)
> You know, that GRAMPUS is an old blowhard! He's
> always complaining about something!

> BRUJON:
> Maybe so, but he's right about one thing. When we
> travel to the feeding grounds Toby's dream sounds
> could attract the Iron Beasts!

> LUMA:
> Yes, but maybe Toby's dream sounds are trying to tell
> us something? Singing whales were once respected, you
> know.

> BRUJON:
> Dreamsingers? Old whale's tales! Those days are gone.
> The Iron Beasts saw to that!

There is an awkward silence.

BRUJON:
Come, Toby. I'm taking you for some breaching lessons.
If you get more exercise, maybe you'll sleep better!

Toby follows his father obediently.

FADE TO:

EXTERIOR - THE MITSU FAMILY GARDEN

Masahiro is clipping trees. Miyoko is feeding fish.

MIYOKO:
MASAHIRO, I know it is your family's tradition, but can
you not find other work to do? It is time to stop killing
whales.

MASAHIRO:
I will not! Don't even think of such things.

MIYOKO:
But...

MASAHIRO:
(cutting her short)
Miyoko! Enough!

In his anger, he accidentally snips off a wrong branch!

MASAHIRO:
Now look what you have made me do!

FADE TO:

UNDER SERENITY BAY - LOOKING OUT TO OPEN SEA

Brujon leads Toby to the edge of the Bay.

BRUJON:
Stick close, TOBY. We're near the open sea now and it
can be very dangerous!
Toby sticks like glue to his father, but is impressed.

TOBY:
Wow! That's amazing!

They swim on cautiously.

BRUJON:
Look, Toby. ... Krill!

Brujon dives deep and shows TOBY how to cast a "bubble net." TOBY watches his father circle, creating a tunnel of bubbles, then expertly swim through it and feed on the krill trapped inside. At the end he does a beautiful breach out of the ocean's surface. Toby tries to imitate the breach but belly-flops awkwardly, scaring away the krill!

>   TOBY:
>   Oooops!

>   BRUJON:
>   Ha! Ha! Don't worry, Toby, I did the same myself when I
>   was your age!

Toby tries several more times but fails each time. This delights a passing school of dolphins.

>   DOLPHINS:
>   (Tittering laughter.)

CUT TO:

C/U OF BRUJON - SURFACE OF THE OCEAN

Brujon briefly feeds alone. Then he turns to Toby.

>   BRUJON:
>   Time to go, Toby.

But Toby is not there! Brujon becomes concerned.

>   BRUJON:
>   Toby?

He sees a flurry of activity in the distance. A number of agitated dolphins are screeching out a warning and just beyond that is a grey noxious mist.

>   BRUJON:
>   The Dark Sea! Toby!

Brujon swims towards them and is relieved to see Toby, too.

>   BRUJON:
>   Toby, what are you doing?

TOBY is close to tears.

>   TOBY:
>   I got confused trying to create bubble nets and got lost!
>   These guys saved me.

BRUJON:
(a little guilty)
I'm sorry. I should have kept an eye on you.

Brujon indicates the grey noxiousness behind them.

BRUJON:
Toby, that is the Dark Sea! Do not EVER go in there! No
one who has swum into it has ever come back!

Toby shudders. Suddenly the dolphins screech a warning. They look and see a dark
ship approaching far away.

BRUJON:
Toby! An Iron Beast!

Toby looks and another cold chill runs through him. A distant explosion is heard. The
dolphins scatter.

BRUJON:
Dive, Toby! Dive!

They dive. But a harpoon follows into the water and explodes.

SFX:
BOOM!

A great volcano of foam bursts up into the air. Toby eventually emerges but Brujon
does not.

TOBY:
Father?

TOBY frantically searches for his father but there is no sign of him. A second
explosion is suddenly heard. Toby panics.

1ST DOLPHIN:
Toby. This way!

Toby follows as a second harpoon explodes behind him.

CUT TO:

BENEATH THE OCEAN SURFACE - SAME MOMENT

Toby follows the dolphins until they are safe.

2ND DOLPHIN:

You must return to the Bay immediately. It is too dangerous for you here.

                         TOBY:
               (alarmed)
               But... my father. I cannot leave without him!

                      3RD DOLPHIN:
               It is too late for him! You must save yourself.

Far above the Iron Beast passes them by.

                        DOLPHIN:
               Let's go! NOW, Toby!

Toby looks around and sees the motionless body of Brujon slowly drifting into the murkiness of the Dark Sea.

                         TOBY:
               Father!

The dolphins force him to turn away and follow them.

                      1ST DOLPHIN:
               Toby. You must save yourself!

Toby resists but is finally ushered away by the dolphins.

CUT TO: INT. – MITSU'S BEDROOM - NIGHT

MITSU sits up in bed and screams.

                         MITSU:
               Aaaahhhhhhhhh! Miyoko enters and gives her daughter
               a "not again" look.

FADE TO:

SERENITY BAY - BENEATH THE SURFACE - DAY

Silent and solemn, Toby and Luma swim. A third young whale swims up to them. It is SEREENA, daughter of Grampus.

                       SEREENA:
               I'm so sorry to hear about your father, Toby.

Toby cannot speak. He swims away. Sereena looks hurt.

                         LUMA:

> Thank you, Sereena, but this is not a good time for us right now. He blames himself for what happened.

                    SEREENA:
I'm sorry. Please forgive me.

She swims away. Luma joins Toby.

                    LUMA:
She just wanted to help, Toby.

                    TOBY:
(tearfully)
I know. But... I just can't forgive myself. I...

                    LUMA:
(interrupting)
Don't talk like that! What happened to your father is not your fault.

                    TOBY:
But it is. I shouldn't have left him. GRAMPUS is right. I am trouble!

                    LUMA:
You are not! GRAMPUS is an old fool!

Luma changes the mood.

                    LUMA:
My grandmother once told me there were whales with incredible voices that could do magical things. They were called DREAMSINGERS. I think your dream sounds are trying to tell us something - tell YOU something,Toby!

But Toby is too hurt to listen.

                    TOBY
I don't care, Mother. Please leave me alone!
Luma watches sadly as her son swims slowly away from her.

DISSOLVE TO:

SURFACE OF THE DARK SEA - DAY

Against a pollution-shrouded sun, silhouetted figures dump more toxic waste containers overboard. The majority sink immediately, but some spill open onto the ocean surface and further foul the already polluted waters.

DISSOLVE TO: BENEATH THE DARK SEA - SAME TIME
The camera follows more meandering waste containers as they
sink. The seabed again creaks and strains as Diomeda pushes up from below.

                         DIOMEDA:
              Aaaarrrrhhbhhhhh!

The seabed holds out but cracks begin to appear.

FADE TO:

LARGE CAVERN IN SERENITY BAY - EARLY EVENING

An old wheezy whale, MAESTRO BALEENI, snoozes at the far end. Baleeni was a one-
time great singer but is now retired and reclusive. Luma enters nervously.

                         LUMA
              Er, Mr. Baleeni?

Baleeni snores. Luma tries again.

                         LUMA
                 (a little louder)
              Mr. Baleeni?

Still no response.

                         LUMA
                 (shouting)
              Mr. Baleeni!

Her voice is so loud it surprises her and echoes around the cavern. It wakes Baleeni!

                         BALEENI
              Wha...? (snort) Eh?

Baleeni grumpily eyes her severely.

                         BALEENI:
                 (disdainfully)
              Yesssssss?

                         LUMA:
              May I have a moment of your time, please?

                         BALEENI:
              Do I know you?

                         LUMA:

My name is Luma. You may have known my husband, Brujon - and our son is Toby.

BALEENI:
(raising an eyebrow)
Toby? Toby? He's the one who makes those awful dream-sounds, isn't he?

TOBY:
(head bowing)
Yes, sir.

Baleeni's laughter ricochets around the cavern walls.

BALEENI:
(trying to stifle his amusement)
Ha! Ha! Ha! (then, recovering) Sorry, Madam. I was not laughing at your son, I was laughing with him! I was amused because I too made strange sounds in my sleep when I was young.

Luma sees a ray of hope.

LUMA:
Then you must understand, Mr.Baleeni?

BALEENI:
Problem?

LUMA:
With my husband gone Grampus has threatened to banish Toby from the pod if his dream sounds don't stop. I thought, if you could just give him singing lessons he...

BALEENI:
(EMPHATIC, interrupting loudly)
Cease! I don't give singing lessons anymore!

LUMA:
But...

BALEENI:
(interrupting again)
Who needs a singer these days? They only bring the earth-walkers to us!

LUMA:
Not even a... Dreamsinger?

Baleeni laughs mockingly. Luma is confused.

LUMA:

I'm glad I amuse you.

BALEENI:

(hard and bitter)

Madame, you come to me unannounced and, quite amazingly, you imagine this noisemaker of yours to be a Dreamsinger! Do you know what it takes to become a Dreamsinger? You waste my time, Madame. I have better things to do with my life!

LUMA:

(narrowing eyes, determined)

Life? What "life" do you speak of, Mr. Baleeni? You have withdrawn from the world. You are a recluse! I was told you had marvelous gifts but all you are is a puffed-up, empty and discontented soul!

His face reveals the truth has hit home.

BALEENI:

(dismissive)

Building song castles in the night sky and singing like a Dreamsinger are two entirely different things. It takes a lot of sacrifice - and pain - to become a Dreamsinger. Most of all it takes that very rare commodity these days... COURAGE!

Luma blinks indignantly at his words.

LUMA:

My son has courage! He is Brujon's son!

Baleeni chooses to ignore her.

BALEENI:

Talent! Hard work! Courage! These are just some of the qualities it takes to be a true Dreamsinger. I doubt your Toby has any of these!

He turns his back on her.

BALEENI:

Now leave!

LUMA:

No, I will not! At least, not until you agree to give him a chance!

BALEENI:
(belligerently)
I will not, Madam.

LUMA:
You will, Sir! I will bring him here tomorrow at sunrise!
And you had better be civil to him... or else!

She swims off before Baleeni can respond further.

FADE TO:

LIVING ROOM - MITSU'S HOME - SUNSET:

Mitsu and her brother Tosumi are dressed for bed. She plays a flute, he a piano.
Miyoko is reading. She looks up.

MIYOKO:
(quietly)
Your father goes back to his ship tomorrow. Mitsu,
could you make your peace with him before he leaves?

Mitsu continues to play.

MIYOKO:
He is an honest and good man who loves us all. He does
what he does for us, so that we might eat and live.

Mitsu stops playing, goes to argue, then thinks better of it.

MIYOKO:
My daughter, it is bedtime. Please at least sleep on it so
you'll be in a good mood when you say goodbye to your
father in the morning. (then to Tosumi) You too,
Tosumi!

Mitsu moves but Tosumi makes a face.

TOSUMI:
(loudly)
Owwww. Do I have to? I never argue with father!

Suddenly another voice barks out from another room.

MASAHIRO:
(off screen)
Bed!

Hearing his father's voice, Tosumi scrambles.

CUT TO:

INT - MITSU'S BEDROOM - SUNSET:

Miyoko tucks Mitsu into bed. Masahiro enters. Miyoko respectfully stands aside.

MASAHIRO:
Goodnight, Mitsu. I will not see you for a while. I hope
we will part as good friends?

Mitsu is torn on how to respond. She thinks. Then she suddenly throws back the
covers and wraps her arms around his neck, holding him tight. Miyoko smiles with
relief.

MITSU:
I am so sorry, my father.

MASAHIRO:
Me too, Mitsu - for hurting you so much with my work.

Masahiro gives her an extra hug. Mitsu looks into his eyes.

MITSU:
Father, please don't go. Not this time.

But Mitsu's plea seems to harden his heart again.

MASAHIRO:
Mitsu, don't start! You know I have no choice. We need
money to live.

Mitsu pleads.

MITSU:
But I don't care if we don't have any money. I'll work!

Masahiro's honor is hurt by the suggestion.

MASAHIRO:
Enough! I am going. Goodnight! Goodbye!

He turns and walks out. Miyoko follows. Mitsu sulkily throws herself back into bed.
Tosumi comes into the bedroom.

TOSUMI
(whispering)
Father is crying! What did you say to him?

MITSU

Nothing! (then, distracted) Tosumi, we've got to stop
him!

FADE OUT:

BENEATH THE DARK SEA - SEA BED

More canisters and toxic waste drift down as the seabed floor arcs up and cracks once
more. A slimy and sinister hand forces its way out of a small crack, scooping up the
slime around it and then pulling it back down again. Diomeda slobbers as he eats.

                    DIOMEDA:
          More! More!

FADE TO:

BALEENI'S CAVERN - DAYTIME

Toby is being examined by Baleeni. He seems unimpressed.

                    BALEENI:
          You expect me to do something with this?

                         LUMA:
                    (resolute)
          I do!

                    BALEENI:
          Hmmmmfffff!

Toby looks distracted. He is still filled with guilt over the loss of his father. Baleeni
seems indifferent to it.

                    BALEENI:
          Show me what you're made of, boy! Sing!

                     TOBY:
          I don't want to! I don't feel like singing! And I won't
          sing!

                    BALEENI:
          Hmmm! You're very much your mother's son, I can see
          that! But I must insist that you sing.

Toby goes to object but his mother interjects.

                     LUMA:
          Toby! This is not about what YOU want. It's about what
          the pod - nay, the world - needs. (then, as an

afterthought) Do this for your father's memory if nothing else!

This does the trick. But Toby's efforts are half-hearted.

TOBY:
(Feeble attempt at singing.)

BALEENI:
Hmmm! As I thought. A complete waste of time!

Luma gives Toby the look of a fearsome mother.

LUMA:
Toby!

He tries one more time. This time there is more effort.

TOBY:
(Slightly better attempt at singing.)
Baleeni listens, then thinks in silence.

BALEENI:
(to Luma)
Very well, I will try. But it will NOT be easy! (then earnestly, to Toby) You have to want to do it, boy! A REAL singer needs to know scales, rhythm, melody, harmony. Each note must have a reason to exist. Must tell a story. A song is a picture. A singer must not only master the music but he must master himself!

Toby shows little enthusiasm. Baleeni continues regardless.

BALEENI:
Nature never lies, boy. Listen to her. Everything she says and does will teach you!

He notes that Toby is still morose.

BALEENI:
(now more sensitively)
Toby, I know you are in pain. It would be unnatural if you did not feel what you feel about your father. But you must rise above it. Let your music carry you. I can give you technique but you have to bring the passion. It is something only found in the soul of a true Dreamsinger! I once...

Baleeni pulls himself up short. He never intended to talk of himself, or Dreamsingers. But Toby shows interest at last.

> TOBY:
> Tell me what you know of Dreamsingers, Mr. Baleeni.

Baleeni is gruff and evasive.

> BALEENI:
> It does not concern you!

> TOBY:
> My mother thinks it does.

> BALEENI:
> Then your mother is wrong!

Toby gives Baleeni the kind of look his mother had earlier.

> TOBY:
> I NEED to know the truth!

Baleeni at last relents.

> BALEENI:
> (resigned)
>
> My family once came from a long line of Dreamsingers. As you know, Dreamsingers were wise and learned whales who could enchant all who heard their songs. All, that is, except the earth-walkers – who killed them off. (There is a glint of anger in his eyes, then he softens again) A Dreamsinger's music was never for entertainment. It was our language, our history, the very soul of our culture – and our existence.

Toby listens intently.

> BALEENI:
> Dreamsingers were our Great Mother's voice, her soul - the greatest singers to have ever been! (then, with a hint of regret and bitterness once more) But they were hunted down and killed by the earth walker's Iron Beasts and are no more! Since then we are all afraid to sing - for fear of bringing the Iron Beasts down upon us again.

> TOBY:
> (eyes watering)
> But? Why did you not become a Dreamsinger, too, Mr. Baleeni?

                              BALEENI :
                        (defensively)
              Me?

                               TOBY:
              Yes, you. You said your family were all Dreamsingers.
              Why not you?

Baleeni suddenly looks sad and vulnerable. He edges back into the shadows.

                              BALEENI:
              Toby, I told you that courage is the most important
              quality a Dreamsinger needs. But courage, I am
              ashamed to say, is what I lacked!

Baleeni is deeply troubled by his admission.

FADE TO:

DOCKS - MITSU'S FATHER'S SHIP - PRE-SUNRISE

The whaling ship is a fearsome, multi-functional, hi-tech killing machine called the
TECHNO SLAYER. It is about to set sail. Mitsu and her brother sneak aboard unseen.

CUT TO:

SERENITY BAY - ABOVE THE SURFACE - SUNRISE
Toby sleeps silently. Nearby other whales sleep peacefully also. Luma whispers to her
sleeping son.

                               LUMA:
              One full moon cycle and still no dream sounds! I am so
              proud, Toby.

At this moment the Moon breaks through the clouds and shines down
on TOBY. He twitches, and whimpers, and...

                               TOBY:
              Howwwwwwweeeeeeellllllllllll!

                               LUMA:
              Oh, no!

Toby is in full-throated dream sound mode.

                               LUMA:
              Toby! Wake up!

But Toby remains entranced and uninhibited.

TOBY:
(louder)
Hooooooowwwwwweeeeeeeellllllllll!

Inevitably the pod wakes up! Grampus first of all.

GRAMPUS:
Wha...??? Not again!

He explodes with anger and shouts in frustration.

GRAMPUS:
E - N - O - U - G - H !!!

The dazed pod gathers behind Grampus. Toby, meanwhile, continues!

GRAMPUS:
That young whale must go! Mark my words, he'll be the
death of us all! We must banish him before we start our
journey!

The pod nods in agreement.

WHALE 1:
He has a point. We are not safe with that noise!

WHALE 2:
Yes, he must be banished! Our lives are at stake!

At this point Toby wakes up, oblivious to everything.

TOBY:
(blinking innocently)
Wha? Did I wake everyone?

He looks around and sees the glowering faces of the pod staring at him. Luma tries to
deflect their anger.

LUMA:
Have you not forgotten? Toby is Brujon's son! Can you
ignore that fact so soon after Brujon's dea...(she stops
herself, knowing Toby is now listening) ...er,
disappearance?

Some members sympathize but Grampus has none of it.

GRAMPUS:
Yes, Toby may be Brujon's son. But remember, if it
wasn't for him, Brujon would still be alive!

Toby is taken aback. The look of guilt consumes him again and he weeps. Some of the pod are uncomfortable with Grampus's lack of tact, especially his own daughter Sereena.

> SEREENA:
> Father! How could you? Brujon's death was not Toby's fault. Leave him alone!
> Grampus gives her a withering look.

> GRAMPUS:
> (imperious)
> We cannot - EVER - sacrifice the safety of the pod for one misfit!

Toby shrinks further into himself. Grampus's withering glare silences all dissent, and he seizes the moment.

> GRAMPUS:
> I move that by the day we start our journey to the feeding grounds, Toby must be gone!

The pod nods its approval. Luma weeps as Sereena swims away in disgust.

FADE TO:

ON BOARD 'TECHNO SLAYER' - MORNING

Under a tarpaulin, MITSU and TOSUMI are concealed in a lifeboat. They are cold and cramped.

> TOSUMI:
> (whining)
> I'm cold - and hungry!

Mitsu hands her brother half a rice cake from her backpack. She eats the other half herself.

> MITSU:
> Here. Now "ssssssh" or else someone will catch us!

The tarpaulin above them lifts up. They are discovered.

> MITSU:
> Oh, shhh.... shoot!

FADE TO:

BALEENI'S CAVERN - MORNING

Dark and shadowy. A clearly shaken Toby enters.

TOBY:
Maestro? Maestro? Are you there?

No response.

TOBY:
Strange?

He is about to leave when he hears Baleeni's voice.

BALEENI:
(feebly)
Toby. Over here!

Toby finds Baleeni nestled in the darkness, strangely quiet.

TOBY:
Maestro! Are you ill?

Baleeni slowly, languidly, raises one eyelid.

BALEENI:
I heard of your troubles, Toby. I am very sorry.

But Toby is more worried about Baleeni.

TOBY:
Maestro, what is wrong?

Baleeni considers his words carefully.

BALEENI:
Toby, what I have told you about Dreamsingers is only part of the story.

Toby's eyes widen.

BALEENI:
There is a deep truth about life. It is simple, but most ignore it.

He pauses, as if to draw inspiration.

BALEENI:
The earth - our Great Mother - is an entire living being
and we all need to live by her rhythms. Sadly, the earth-
walkers do not fully realize this yet and so they must

learn. They still act as if the world is theirs to use as they want. It is a grave mistake, Toby, a grave mistake!

He has to pause for breath.

> BALEENI:
> The ancient Dreamsingers knew this, Toby, and it was their purpose to pass this knowledge on, through their songs. But the earth-walkers slayed them and so they never learned.

BALEENI pauses again.

> BALEENI:
> When your mother brought you to me I was reluctant to take you on. I sensed you were much troubled deep inside. I didn't think you were up to the task!

He suddenly finds strength and purpose in his words.

> BALEENI:
> Toby, what lies ahead of you is not easy. A true singer - a DREAMSINGER - needs to look deep inside and have the courage to face the darkness that is there. In doing this we confront our greatest fears. That is what you must do!

> TOBY:
> But you will help me, won't you?

> BALEENI:
> Alas, I am old and my time is almost up.

> TOBY:
> (almost tearful)
> No!

> BALEENI:
> Yes, Toby. But do not weep, for I am content in my belief that I have found a true Dreamsinger to carry on our tradition.

Toby is suddenly nervous to have this responsibility.

> BALEENI:
> There is a legend - an old, old legend - that when the world is in its greatest peril a young Dreamsinger will emerge to save her. I believe that is you, Toby!

                    TOBY:
              (genuinely doubting)
            No. I don't think so.

                    BALEENI:
            But I do. You have many of the right qualities. But, as
            yet, you don't have them all!

                    TOBY:

            What must I do?

                    BALEENI:
            This I alone cannot tell you. But you will be shown your
            way as you swim the oceans alone. Keep your eyes and
            ears open. And above all, listen with your heart - to the
            wind, the waves, the birds. The Great Mother herself
            will reveal it all to you if you have the ears to hear and
            the eyes to see.

Now Baleeni is tired.

                    BALEENI:
            Now you must go! These old bones of mine are very tired.

                    TOBY:
            Maestro? How can I ever repay you?

                    BALEENI
              (smiling weakly)
            You already have, Toby! You already have!

FADE TO:

SERENITY BAY - DAY

The day of the great journey! The entire pod is assembled for the trek to the southern
feeding grounds. Toby watches from afar, wishing he were with them. Luma swims to
him.

                    LUMA:
            Please, let me stay with you.

                    TOBY:
(sounding more brave than he really is)
            No, Mother. I have to face whatever I need to face alone.
            My greatest fear!

                    LUMA:
            Your greatest fear? Do you know what it is?

TOBY:
No. But being alone will be my best way of finding it out,
I reckon!

LUMA:
Then promise me you will stay in sight of the pod - and
that you will never, EVER enter the Dark Sea!

TOBY nods. Suddenly the pod, immense and powerful, begins to head south. LUMA
reluctantly joins them.

LUMA:
Farewell, my son. Take care!

Slowly, determinedly, the pod recedes from sight. Toby is alone. He attempts to
breach with exaggerated bravado but again fails with a belly flop. Coughing and
spluttering, he sees Sereena watching. Embarrassed, he goes to leave.

SEREENA:
Toby... wait!

Toby turns as Sereena catches up with him.

SEREENA:
I couldn't leave without saying goodbye.

TOBY:
Does your father know you're here?

SEREENA:
No. But I want to apologize for him. He was very cruel in
the way he spoke about you.

TOBY:
I guess he had his reasons. (then, with self-doubt in his
voice) He's probably right anyway!

SEREENA:
Don't say that. It's not true!

TOBY:
You know, I wish I could believe that.

Toby looks sad as he swims off.

SEREENA:
I won't forget you, Toby.

She swims off and Toby casts one longing look back to her.

TOBY:
(to himself)
And I won't forget you, either, Sereena.

FADE TO:

CAPTAIN'S CABIN - LATER

Mitsu, Tosumi and Masahiro stand before the furious Captain. He studies them impassively. Masahiro looks humbled.

MASAHIRO:
I'm sorry. I had no idea they were aboard.

The Captain blows a perfect smoke ring, then he sucks it back in. He coldly puffs it out again into Masahiro's face.

CAPTAIN:
I hate kids! If I had my way I would throw them to the
sharks, or boil them in whale blubber!

Masahiro has never seen the Captain so enraged.

MITSU:
(with contempt)
My father knew nothing of this!

CAPTAIN:
Silence!

TOSUMI:
(squeaky, with fear)
It was my sister's idea!

The Captain ignores him and points a bony finger to Masahiro.

CAPTAIN:
I hold you responsible, Masahiro! These chimps of yours
must be punished. Shall I throw them to the sharks?

Tosumi edges behind his father nervously.

CAPTAIN:
Hmmmf! Take them to your cabin while I decide what to
do with them.

He turns his back and stubs out his cigarette on the desk. Masahiro hurries the kids out of the room. The Captain takes out a hip flask and slugs long and hard. He then slumps into a chair and lights up another cigarette.

CAPTAIN:
Brats!

FADE TO:

SURFACE OF TECHNO SLAYER - SAME MOMENT

A sailor throws repulsive garbage over the side. It hits the water, floats momentarily, then sinks out of sight.

DISSOLVE TO:

OCEAN BENEATH THE TECHNO SLAYER - SAME MOMENT

More garbage descends in the Dark Sea. The seabed appears worse than ever. Diomeda's sinewy hand is working at the crack in the seabed, seeking liberation. MUTANT SEA CREATURES -pale and almost lifeless sharks - now hover in anticipation.

DIOMEDA:
Grrroooowwwwlllllllll!!! Thank you!

FADE TO:

BENEATH THE SURFACE OF THE OPEN SEA - NIGHT

TOBY swims alone in the open sea. He is tired and hungry. Eerie moonlight filters through and creates a spooky scene.

TOBY:
I am not afraid! I am not afraid! I am not afraid!

He snuggles into a discreet cave and tries to sleep. Suddenly there is a vibrating, ethereal light that resonates all around him. It builds and builds. He is eventually bathed in a soft, warm glow; yet, strangely, he feels no fear.

CUT TO:

CABIN ON BOARD THE TECHNO SLAYER - SAME MOMENT

Mitsu sleeps above her brother in a double bunk bed. The mysterious white glow resonates above Mitsu, too.

CUT TO:

BOTTOM OF OPEN SEA - NIGHT:

Toby begins to float upward, drawn by the mysterious light. He hovers in the soft, warm light, just above the surface of the water. A wise and kindly female voice speaks to him.

FEMALE VOICE:

Greetings, Toby!

Toby squints in the brightness of the light.

TOBY:

Who are you?

Noting his discomfort, somebody reduces intensity of the Light. This reveals a radiant white form of the 'spirit whale, ' THES.

FEMALE VOICE:
(grandly)
I am called THES. I am honored to meet you, young man.

TOBY:

What do you want of me?

THES:

Your attention!

TOBY:

Are you a ghost?

THES:

A ghost? (Chuckle) No, I am not a ghost, exactly.

Toby looks blankly.

THES

I am sent as a messenger of the Great Mother. I am here to help you! (then, suddenly more serious) Do you know of the Dark Sea?

TOBY:

Yes. My parents warned me never to go there. (then sadly, guiltily) My father was lost to it!

THES:

Why do you blame yourself for his fate? It was not your fault. It was his destiny!

TOBY:

If I had gone back for him he might still be here today!

THES:

No, there was nothing you could have done. You are too hard on yourself, Toby. You are not at fault! It would hurt him to know you are thinking this way!

Toby tries to absorb what she has said. Tears form in his eyes as the guilt visibly begins to lift from him.

                              TOBY:
          What do I need to do?

                              THES:
          Enter the Dark Sea!

                              TOBY:
               (suddenly very fearful)
          What? No!

Thes senses the fear.

                              THES:
          Let me tell you about it. I think you will see why it is
          necessary for you to do this.

As Thes talks we see a MONTAGE sequence of what is being said.

DISSOLVE TO:

MONTAGE SEQUENCE - AS PER DIALOGUE

                              THES:
(v.o.)
          The Dark Sea wasn't always a Dark Sea. Long ago it was a place of color
          and beauty. Life was abundant. But then came the earth-walkers!

A cold chill runs through Toby.

                              TOBY:
          The earth-walkers?

                              THES:
          Yes, as with many things, a number of the earth-walkers took what was
          good and left it bad.

                              TOBY
               (v.o.)
          Are they evil?

                              THES:
               (v.o.)
          No, they are not evil, Toby. The earth-walkers are complicated
          creatures. They have all the brilliance to make our world a true heaven
          on earth. But as often happens, some of them are self-seeking and go
          too far. At this moment in time a terrible force
          grows within the heart of the Great Mother that threatens to destroy

everything as a result of the earth-walkers' neglect. Since the beginning of time this unspeakable force has been kept in check. But now the earth-walkers have changed
all that and all of existence will soon be in peril!

TOBY:
Gasp! But what has this to do with me?

THES:
Day by day, hour by hour, the earth-walkers pour acidic poisons into the Dark Sea, opening up a gaping wound in the Great Mother's flesh and allowing this powerful force, DIOMEDA, to escape.

TOBY:
But why do they do this?

THES:
They do not know they do this, Toby!

Toby frowns.

THES:
I can see that I will have to show you. Are you prepared for an amazing journey?

TOBY nods, nervously.

THES:
Very well, but I have to borrow your voice. Do you have any objections?

TOBY:
No.

THES:
Good. Now relax and harmonize with me.

Thes intones a beautiful musical note. Toby attempts to imitate it, and finally does so. Toby's spirit body lifts from his physical one. Shocked, Toby stops singing.

TOBY:
(in panic) Arhhhhhhhh!

But Thes reassures him.

THES:
Don't fight it, Toby! Swim with the Spirit! No harm will come to you.

Toby intones the note once more and his spirit body rises up with Thes. They fly upwards, into the night sky. Once they are rising Thes stops their singing and Toby discovers to his delight that he can still fly.

> TOBY:
> I'm flying, Thes! I'm actually flying

> THES:
> Indeed you are. Come, Toby, this night holds many
> surprises for you!

CUT TO:

CABIN ON THE TECHNO SLAYER - NIGHT

Mitsu is still in bed. The glow that is on her face now spreads to her whole body. Her spirit body rises up and floats through the cabin wall.

CUT TO:

EXTERIOR WHALING SHIP - NIGHT

Mitsu's spirit body rises up from the ship and into the starry night sky.

CUT TO:

SKY ABOVE THE EARTH ~ NIGHT

Thes teaches Toby how to control his flight.

> THES:
> Turn your head in the direction you want to go. Like
> this. See?

Thes motions his head to the right and he flies to the right. TOBY follows his example. He sees the spirit body of Mitsu rising up towards him.

> TOBY:
> An earth-walker!

He panics and begins to fall. Thes moves beneath him and stops him from falling.

> THES:
> I told you there would be surprises!

Toby regains his composure and is a little less frightened.

> THES:
> Toby, not all of the earth-walkers wish to harm you.
> This child loves you more than you will ever know.

TOBY looks nervously towards MITSU. She smiles at him warmly.

>   THES:
> Toby, this child is Mitsu. She is your friend. Can she ride
> on your back?

Toby looks uncertain.

>   TOBY:
> Er... I suppose so!

Mitsu smiles.

>   MITSU:
> Thank you.

Thes directs them towards a distant land mass.

>   THES:
> Let me show you two the wonders of the Great Mother
> at first hand. Hold on!

They accelerate and enter daylight time. They pass continents, oceans, mountains, deserts and jungles - and are in awe of the breathtaking beauty of it all.

>   TOBY:
> Oh, I never knew. It's so beautiful!

>   MITSU
> Yes, it is!

>   THES:
> Here you see the oneness of our creation. Everything is
> dependent on everything else. The Great Mother is a
> living, breathing being. The forests are her lungs. The
> rivers and oceans are her bloodstream.

>   TOBY
> Wow!

>   MITSU:
> I didn't realize!

>   THES:
> So far you have seen the world of Nature, my friends.
> Let me now show you the world of Man.

Thes leads them towards a city. A grayish/purple cloud hovers above it ominously. They fly straight into it.

TOBY:
Cough! Cough! What is this stuff?

MITSU:
Pollution!

THES:
Yes, one of Man's great contributions to life! It poisons the air and infects the breath of the Great Mother.

Toby begins to look sick. Thes takes them lower.

TOBY:
It's so noisy!

MITSU:
You get used to it!

THES:
So much noise that Nature's song is lost!

TOBY:
I hate it!

Mitsu bows her head briefly. She is ashamed of it.

THES:
Yet even in all this chaos there are those who still hear the song. They sing and pray and dream of better things. Like MITSU here!

Toby looks down to the city and frowns.

TOBY:
I don't get it! Why would anyone want to live like this?

MITSU:
We just don't know the truth any more, Toby. We are not taught that.

But Toby has had enough.

TOBY:
Please take me away from this!

Thes complies. They ascend again.

THES:
Now do you see why the Great Mother is in so much pain?

                    MITSU:
I am so sorry.

                    THES:
Even now some terrible thing is stirring that few are
aware of!

                    TOBY:
Diomeda?

                    THES:
A beast that feeds off ignorance! Come, I will show you.

Thes whisks them away. Toby and Mitsu's heads spin. They clench their eyes tightly
shut.

CUT TO:

CABIN ON THE TECHNO SLAYER - NIGHT

Mitsu's sleeping body speaks.

MITSU (in her sleep)
Arrrrrgggggghhhh!

CUT TO:

STAR-FILLED CONSTELLATIONS - ABOVE THE EARTH

They travel slower now. Toby is thoughtful.

                    TOBY
          Thes?

                    THES
          Yes?

                    TOBY:
What do I have to do to become a Dreamsinger?

                    THES:
Exactly what you have done. Exactly what you are
doing.

                    TOBY:
But something must be missing, otherwise I would be a
Dreamsinger already.

                    THES:

That is true, Toby. You have yet to find your TRUE
VOICE!

                    TOBY:
My True Voice? What is that?

                    THES:
When you overcome your greatest fear, then your heart
will open and your True Voice will emerge.

                    TOBY:
But what is my greatest fear?

Thes looks at him in great seriousness.

                    THES:
I think you already know!

                    TOBY:
            (thinking, realizing, then nervously)
The Dark Sea?

                    THES:
Even more. You must face the beast that lurks within
the Dark Sea!

                    TOBY:
Diomeda?

Toby shakes with fear. Mitsu senses it.

                    MITSU:
But what can I do?

                    THES:
You must help Toby through his fear.

                    THES:
He will sense you with him, even when you are not
there. Will you do that?

                    MITSU:
            (eagerly)
Yes!

Meanwhile, Toby is still trying to work things out.

                    TOBY:
But... the Dark Sea? No one who's entered it has ever
returned!

                    THES:
That's true!

TOBY is now very frightened.

                    TOBY:
But I...!

                    THES:
          (interrupting)
You are scared?

                    TOBY:
Yes. (then, head bowed) I am scared!

                    THES:
Then there begins your greatest fear, Toby. If you want
to become a Dreamsinger you must face it!

                    TOBY:
But... I promised... my father!

                    THES:
Toby, if you risk nothing you gain nothing. Maybe you
can save him, too?

                    TOBY:
But he's de... (then, ashamed) I don't think that I could
ever enter the Dark Sea - ever!

                    THES:
Then I'm afraid you will fail your life's purpose, Toby,
and the world will go the way of your father. Do you
want to carry such a burden all of your life?

                    TOBY:
No. But you ask too much of me.

                    THES:
No more than you can bear.

Toby thinks.

                    TOBY:
No, I cannot do it. Even if I could, how could I defeat
Diomeda?

                    THES:

> Diomeda is an all-powerful beast, yes. But he can be
> defeated. He is powerless against the song of a
> Dreamsinger!

Toby's eyes widen.

                    TOBY:
> But I am not a Dreamsinger. I want to go back to where I
> came from!

Thes does not want to force Toby against his will.

                    THES:
> As you wish, Toby. But there is one last thing I must
> show you. It will not be pleasant, I'm afraid!

Thes guides Toby and Mitsu down towards the Earth. Gliding across the open sea, they encounter an Iron Beast.

                    MITSU:
>   (shocked)
> A whaling ship!

They travel in close as the ship makes a kill. Toby and Mitsu are sickened by what they see.

                    TOBY:
> I cannot watch!

                    MITSU:
> Gasp! Oh, no!

The shock of it all is too much. They immediately feel their spirit selves being sucked back towards their bodies. As they spiral down they hear the voice of Thes.

                    THES:
> Remember, Toby, you can stop these things from
> happening. You can change all this. Mitsu and I will help
> you.

DISSOLVE TO:

CABIN ON THE TECHNO SLAYER - NIGHT:

MITSU's spirit body crashes into her sleeping body. She sits up in her bed in horror of what she has seen.

                    MITSU:
>   (Scream!)
> MASAHIRO wakes up and goes to comfort her.

MASAHIRO:
It is all right, my daughter. It was only another dream.

MITSU rubs her eyes as she is reminded of what she has seen.

MITSU:
No. I'm afraid that it was all too real!

Typically, Tosumi sleeps through it all.

DISSOLVE TO:

BOTTOM OF THE OPEN SEA

Toby opens his eyes to see that he is back again. He shakes with the horror he has seen. In his head he hears Thes.

THES:
(v.o. - fading)
Seek your True Voice, Toby, and all will be well. The child and I will help you. Swim with the spirit, Toby. Swim with the spirit!

FADE TO:

CABIN ON THE TECHNO SLAYER - SUNRISE

MITSU wakes up before anyone. She looks out of the porthole and sees that the sun is rising.

MITSU
This all has to end!

Mitsu tiptoes out of the cabin. She sneaks past a sailor on deck and makes straight for her father's harpoon gun. Quickly and nimbly she turns the screws on the sighting mechanism and then returns to bed as if nothing has happened.

FADE TO:

OPEN SEA - LATER

Toby is swimming far behind the pod, coming to terms with what has happened. He is deep in thought. He sees a strange and sad-eyed dolphin who looks lost.

TOBY:
Hello. My name's Toby. Are you alone, too?

The dolphin is spaced-out but friendly.

CHETLY:

(like a pot-head)
Alone, dude? Hmmmmmm? Who's alone?

TOBY:

Then where's the rest of your pod?

CHETLY:

School, dude. We call it a school. (pause) I dropped out
long ago!

TOBY:

Why? It's rare to see a dolphin swimming alone.

CHETLY:

I might say the same about a young whale. What's up?

TOBY:

I've been banished!

CHETLY:

Banished? Like they dumped you, man? Gee, you must
have done something real bad.

TOBY:

I couldn't help it. I sang in my sleep.

CHETLY:

They banished you for singing in your sleep?. Gee, that's
harsh! Where are you off to now?

TOBY:

I'm looking for my True Voice.

CHETLY:

Hey. I know just the place you'll find it, Toby. The Dark
Sea. You'll find whatever you want there!

TOBY:

(alarmed)
Gasp! You've been there - and come back?

CHETLY:

Didn't say that, dude. But there's always a first time for
everything, right? I'm told things are cool there, if you
know where to look.

TOBY:

My father always told me that nobody who's ever been
there has come back to tell the tale!

CHETLY:
Maybe because it's so good that nobody wants to leave?
Wanna check it out?

TOBY:
My father's there and never came back. I'm scared!

CHETLY:
No need for that, dude. I'm told there's a place there
called THE GLOW! Once it lights you up...Well, you'll
love it, dude. I hear you'll never want to come back once
you see it! Perhaps your dad's there, man?

TOBY:
You think?

CHETLY:
Maybe. Bet that's where you can find your True Voice,
though!

TOBY:
I'm not so sure.

CHETLY:
Well, if you don't go for it I guess you'll never know,
man!

Chetly swims off, leaving Toby pondering.

TOBY:
The Glow. I wonder?

FADE TO:

ANOTHER LOCATION IN THE OPEN SEA - SOME TIME LATER

Toby is swimming far behind the pod and sees krill. Again he tries to create a bubble
net to catch them, the way his father showed him. He starts well. Bubbles rise to the
surface forming a net around the krill. But just as he is about to begin his upward
ascent to get them he notices Sereena is watching him. He loses his concentration,
misses the krill and gulps in empty sea water! A wave of shrimp spills over his face -
he has forgotten to open his mouth! She wants to laugh but doesn't.

SEREENA:
Hi. Remember me?

Toby tries to maintain some kind of dignity.

TOBY:
(awkwardly, but excited)

Yes - Sereena!

                    SEREENA:
If my father knew I was here, he'd skin me alive!

                    TOBY:
But you came anyway?

                    SEREENA:
I was worried about you.

                    TOBY:
          (mock bravado)
Oh you don't need to worry about me. I can take care of
myself!

                    SEREENA:
So I noticed. You must still be pretty hungry.

                    TOBY:
          (chagrined)
You saw?

                    SEREENA:
          (laughing)
I'm sorry I distracted you!

They both giggle. Suddenly a booming voice intrudes.

                    GRAMPUS:
Sereena! What are you doing here?

                    SEREENA:
          (startled)
Father! I... I just wanted to see if Toby was all right!

                    GRAMPUS:
Sereena, how dare you disobey me! This whale is
banished!

                    TOBY:
          (courageously)
Sir, she is not a child anymore.

                    GRAMPUS:
Silence! Sereena, get back to the pod immediately. I
forbid you to see this whale again!

                    SEREENA:
But Daddy. I...

GRAMPUS:
(almost screeching)
Go!

Sereena reluctantly departs - but not without giving a parting "I'm sorry" glance to Toby.

GRAMPUS:
This is a last warning. Stay away from Sereena - and stay away from the pod. You are nothing but trouble.

TOBY:
I... Oh, never mind!

Toby turns and swims dejectedly away. He begins to sing defiantly as he goes. Grampus returns to the pod. Suddenly, a deep and terrifying cry of pain is heard far away.

DISSOLVE TO:

BOTTOM OF THE DARK SEA - SAME TIME

The grotesque form of Diomeda is now more visible through the widening crack. The mutant sharks watch in entranced awe.

DIOMEDA:
Arrrrhhhhh! That sound! That sound! I cannot bear it!

The Mutant Sea Creatures look on in bewilderment. They cannot hear what Diomeda hears.

DIOMEDA:
Aaarrrrrrhhhhhhhhhhhh!

Diomeda resumes his frantic struggles to release himself.

FADE TO:

CABIN ON THE "TECHNO SLAYER" - SAME DAY

Mitsu and Tosumi stand with their father on deck. Masahiro and Tosumi look for whales but Mitsu sulkily doesn't.

MASAHIRO:
This is the time of year when the whales head south to their summer feeding grounds. We should see them soon.

MITSU:
Hmmmmfffff!

Masahiro continues ~ ignoring his daughter.

> MASAHIRO:
> It seems one solitary whale has already been spotted
> swimming near here. The captain is tracking it now.

Mitsu is suddenly alarmed.

> MITSU:
> (whispering to herself, a tear welling up)
> Gasp! No! Don't let it be Toby!

FADE TO

BENEATH THE OPEN SEA - SAME DAY

Toby hears a peculiar kind of singing. We will soon discover it comes from a strange-
looking crab, CRUSTY.

> CRUSTY:
> (singing, blues style)
> I got the seabed blues. Down here the water moves so
> slow. Yeah. I got the seabed blues. Down here the water
> moves so slow. When you reach rock bottom, you're
> about as low as you can go.

Toby sees two beady, white eyes peering out from a dark rock cranny. CRUSTY stops
singing and eases himself out.

> CRUSTY:
> Whoa! What do we have here?

> TOBY:
> I'm Toby.

> CRUSTY:
> Hmmm. Pleasure's all mine. Crusty's my name. Singing's
> my game.

> TOBY:
> Then maybe you can help me? I'm looking for my True
> Voice.

> CRUSTY:
> Hmmmmm? Don't rightly know where you'll find that.
> How'd you lose it in the first place?

> TOBY:
> You don't lose your True voice -you find it!

> CRUSTY:

Shucks, don't rightly know how you can find something without losing it first? (shaking his head) Weird. Still, I wish you luck, friend.

                        CRUSTY

Me, I'm just a "blues" kinda guy, myself.

                        TOBY:

Blues? Dreamsingers sing in colors. You must have found your own True Voice, then?

                        CRUSTY:

Hmmmmm? Maybe I have, maybe I haven't. Only got color one though! Say, what's a 'Dreamsinger'?

                        TOBY:

Dreamsingers sing in all kinds of shapes and colors, so I'm told.

CRUSTY looks at TOBY as if he is mad.

                        CRUSTY:

Shapes and colors? Holy moly! You been to The Glow or something?

TOBY's eyes widen.

                        TOBY:

The Glow? In the Dark Sea? What do you know about The Glow? I hear you can get whatever you want there?

                        CRUSTY:

Yea, an' maybe some things you don't want, too!

                        TOBY:

What do you mean?

                        CRUSTY:

Well, word has it The Glow's a mighty mean place. If you want my advice, don't you go messing around there. It'll scramble your brain!

                        TOBY:
                    (suddenly apprehensive)
Oh no!

                        CRUSTY:

What's up Tobe?

                        TOBY:

My father - he might be there! I have to save him!

                    CRUSTY:
Uh-oh. Take my word for it, if he's there he ain't gonna
flow no mo'! Better save yourself. It's too late for him!

                    TOBY:
No... I... (then, thinking) I have to save him! Thanks,
Crusty. You've been a big help.

                    CRUSTY:
Sure thing. Hope you get your pa before The Glow gets
you!

                    TOBY:

I'll try.

                    CRUSTY:
And if you see any of those Dreamsingers you're on
about – tell 'em Crusty says hello. Maybe we can all sing
some colors together some time?

CRUSTY crawls back to his hole, singing as he goes.

                    CRUSTY:
I got the seabed blues. Down here the water moves so
slow. Yeah. I got the seabed blues. Down here the water
moves so slow...

                    TOBY:
        (joining in)
...when you reach rock bottom, you're 'bout as low as
you can go.

                    CRUSTY:
        (looking back and smiling)
Hmmmm-mmmmm! Now that's music to my ears, Tobe!

                    TOBY:
See you around, Crusty.

Toby swims upward again, towards the sunlight. As he surfaces he fails to notice the
Techno Slayer stealing up behind him.

CUT TO:

BRIDGE OF THE TECHNO SLAYER - SAME MOMENT

The drinking Captain sees a blip on his radar screen. He surveys the horizon and sees
Toby.

CAPTAIN:
(slurred)
Whale! Whale straight ahead! Man the harpoon, you
lazy slobs!

There is a wild scramble as crewmen prepare. Mitsu is alarmed. She pleads with her father.

MITSU:
Don't, Father! That's my whale! It's Toby!

But Masahiro pushes her away and races to the harpoon. Tosumi is excited by the action.

TOSUMI:
Mitsu, are we going to see a whale shoot?

Mitsu casts a look of scorn at her brother.

CUT TO:

SURFACE OF THE OPEN SEA - SAME MOMENT

Toby remains oblivious. He looks isolated and vulnerable on the surface. Suddenly, he senses danger and turns to see the ship. He tries to escape but the ship closes fast.

CUT TO .....

DECK OF THE TECHNO SLAYER - SAME MOMENT

Masahiro prepares to fire the harpoon gun. Mitsu runs over and tries to stop him from shooting. Under the Captain's gaze Masahiro holds her back.

CAPTAIN:
You men, grab those kids! Keep them away from the
gun!

The children are held by two burly sailors.

CUT TO:

SURFACE OF THE OPEN SEA - SAME MOMENT

Toby swims frantically but the ship closes in on him.

CUT TO:

DECK OF THE TECHNO SLAYER - SAME MOMENT

Masahiro carefully aims the harpoon gun at the easy target of Toby swimming ahead of the ship. Mitsu screams to him.

                              MITSU:
                    No, Father. Don't!

Through the view-finder the gun is perfectly aligned with TOBY. Masahiro's finger tightens on the trigger and the harpoon gun fires.

                              SFX
                    Boom!

CUT TO:

SURFACE OF THE OPEN SEA - SAME MOMENT

Toby freezes when he hears the harpoon gun fire. He freezes for the impact. However, thanks to Mitsu's tampering of the gun's mechanism it hits the ocean way off-target!

CUT TO:

DECK OF THE TECHNO SLAYER - SAME MOMENT

Masahiro looks in disbelief. MITSU cheers with joy.

                         MASAHIRO:
                    (glaring at his daughter)
                    This was your work!

The Captain screams in a fierce rage.

                          CAPTAIN:
                    Fools! Imbeciles! Masahiro, wait till I get my hands on
                    those little brats of yours!

Mitsu and Tosumi look scared - Tosumi most of all. The boy struggles free and makes a dash for it. He loses his footing on nearby ropes and plunges overboard!

                          TOSUMI:
                    Aaaaarrrrhhhhh!

The child hits the sea. The Captain curses and takes another swig. A lifeboat is lowered as Tosumi struggles in the water.

                          TOSUMI:
                    Help me! (gurgle) Help... (gurgle)...me!

CUT TO:

SURFACE OF THE OPEN SEA - SAME MOMENT

Toby sees the boy struggling in the water and Mitsu crying for him. His compassion kicks in. He dives. He surfaces under Tosumi, balancing the flailing child on his back.

CUT TO:

DECK OF THE 'TECHNO SLAYER' - SAME MOMENT

All are in disbelief as they stare at Toby with the boy on his back. The lifeboat reaches them and Tosumi is rescued. The Captain is unmoved.

>   CAPTAIN:
>   Well, what are you waiting for? Shoot the whale! Shoot
>   the whale!

Everyone exchanges looks. Mitsu is outraged.

>   MITSU:
>   No! Father! NO!

Masahiro reluctantly readjusts the sights on the gun. He prepares for another shot. Mitsu's eyes fill with tears.

>   MITSU:
>   Father! Please?

Masahiro looks into her eyes and his heart melts. He turns the gun away from Toby.

>   MASAHIRO:
>   This time he is safe, Mitsu. But only this time!

He turns to face the Captain to see what his punishment will be. The Captain is furious. But when he sees the looks on the rebellious faces of Masahiro, Mitsu, Tosumi and the rest of the crew, he backs off.

>   CAPTAIN:
>   Masahiro! My office!

FADE TO:

BENEATH THE OPEN SEA - SAME MOMENT

Toby dives and hides among the rocks. He shakes as he watches the dark, ominous shadow of the Techno Slayer passing over him.

FADE TO:

BRIDGE OF THE TECHNO SLAYER - SHORTLY AFTERWARDS

Masahiro stands awkwardly, head bowed. The CAPTAIN paces up and down, incessantly puffing his cigarette. He grinds it out on his desk and immediately lights a new one.

CAPTAIN:
So, Masahiro Kudo, what am I to do with you?

Masahiro shuffles awkwardly.

CAPTAIN:
Where once you were dependable, now you are no better than your despicable children!

MASAHIRO:
Captain, with all respect, that whale saved my child.

There is venom in the Captain's face.

CAPTAIN:
A whale is a whale in my world! None of this would have happened if you'd controlled your brats in the first place. (then, with a sneering contempt) Get back to your harpoon and NEVER fail me again!

MASAHIRO:
(muttering)
Yes, sir.

CAPTAIN:
What did you say?

MASAHIRO
(louder)
I said "yes, sir."

Masahiro bows and moves towards his post.

CAPTAIN:
And send your children to me. From now on they stay with me here, where I can keep an eye on them!

Masahiro stops and goes to protest. However he sees the anger in his Captain's eyes and thinks better of it.

MASAHIRO:
Yes, sir.

He exits rapidly.

FADE TO:

THE OPEN SEA - SHORTLY AFTER

Toby surfaces and takes a deep gulp of air. In the distance, the Techno Slayer can be seen slowly sailing away. A new terrifying thought suddenly comes to him.

TOBY:
The Pod!

He scans the horizon and swims off in pursuit of the ship. For comfort, he sings as he goes.

CUT TO:

BOTTOM OF THE DARK SEA - SAME TIME

Diomeda is further revealed. His grotesque, slimy head now emerges from the widening crack. He roars and grabs his ears, as if agonized. He cries out in anger and pain.

> DIOMEDA:
> Arrrrhhhhhh! That noise!

The other mutant sea creatures are still confused. Their leader, MURDO, awaits orders.

> DIOMEDA:
> I want the maker of that noise! NOW! Bring him to me!

> MURDO:
> (unsure)
> Right. Sure thing, Boss!

> DIOMEDA:
> Fail and I'll throw you to The Glow. All of you!

Murdo takes him seriously. They scrabble around in all directions, but are not sure where to go first.

FADE TO:

SKIRTING THE DARK SEA - DUSK

Toby swims in search of the pod as a filmy mist hangs in the water. For courage he continues to sing. He soon becomes tired and eventually settles down to sleep.

DISSOLVE TO:

SAME SCENE - DAWN

Toby is singing in his sleep. A sinister shadow suddenly crosses over him.

MURDO:
(v.o.)
Great set of pipes you have there, kid!

Toby wakes up. He's surrounded by mutant sharks. They stare at him with grinning, menacing teeth.

1ST WHALE:
Yeah, that's some voice yer have there.

2ND WHALE:
A real piece of work.

They all nod and grin. Toby looks scared.

MURDO:
(hardly reassuring)
It's OK. Nothing to be afraid of. What's your name?

TOBY:
Toby.

MURDO:
Toby. That's nice.

The others smile and nod in agreement.

1ST WHALE:
Real nice. Eh, Murdo?

MURDO winks.

MURDO:
What are you doing out here all alone?

TOBY:
I... I'm looking for my True Voice.

MURDO:
(with fake sympathy)
Aw, that's nice. Hey fellas, maybe we could help Toby
find his True Voice, huh?

They all laugh, flashing their razor sharp teeth.

2ND WHALE:
Sure, Boss. It'd be an honor!

TOBY:

(uncertain)
It's OK, really. I wouldn't want to put you guys out.

MURDO:
Hey, no problem! It can be really dangerous around
here. We wouldn't want you to get into any trouble -
would we, guys?

ALL WHALES:
Of course not, Boss!

MURDO looks to his companions and they all laugh. Toby acknowledges them with a
weak smile. They move off, but Toby pulls back. They nudge him towards the Dark
Sea.

TOBY:
(increasingly nervous)
Er... this can't be right?

MURDO:
Toby, trust us. We know this place like the back of our
fin. Relax!

They surround him close and drive him forward into the murky darkness of that Dark
Sea.

MURDO:
And anyway, we want to introduce you to our boss. He's
real interested in you!

Toby looks as if he is in his worst nightmare - which of course he is!

FADE TO:

ELSEWHERE BENEATH THE OPEN SEA - DAY

The pod moves gracefully southward. Sereena swims with Luma at the back of the
procession.

SEREENA:
I am sure TOBY's all right. We'll see him soon.

LUMA:
(looking back, fretfully)
But it's been many days since I saw him.

SEREENA:
Don't worry. I'm sure that he will return to us safely.

Sereena sounds confident but she also casts back a concerned glance when Luma is not looking.

FADE TO:

BENEATH THE DARK SEA - DAY

Murdo and his gang lead Toby further into the Dark Sea. The mutant whales are upbeat, whereas Toby is filled with fear.

                    MURDO:
          Relax, Toby. Look around you. This isn't all that bad!
          Wait till you see The Glow! That's really something!
          Huh, guys?

The others snigger.

                    1ST WHALE:
              (sarcastically)
          Yeah. Whatever!

                    MURDO:
          Huh?

                    1ST WHALE:
          Er, whatever you say boss!

Toby looks around for an escape route. Murdo notices.

                    MURDO:
          Not trying to leave us, are you, Toby? The boss really
          wouldn't like that. I mean, we wouldn't want to hurt
          you. And I know he wants you back in one piece! (then,
          as an aside to the others) Or two, or three, at the very
          least!

He chops his jaws together a few times to emphasize the point. The all laugh and continue swimming.

FADE TO:

CAPTAIN'S BRIDGE ON THE TECHNO SLAYER - DAY:

The air is filled with smoke as the Captain paces nervously. The door opens and Mitsu and Tosumi are pushed in.

                    CAPTAIN:
          Sit! (then, glaring) And don't move!

They sit reluctantly. The Captain mutters as he works.

> CAPTAIN:
> You two have done enough damage already. (then,
> turning to them aggressively) There will be no more!

He surveys the sea from the bridge window. Beside him there is the sonar device that picks up whales beneath the surface.

> MITSU:
> Can't we come over and see what you're doing?

The Captain scowls, then relents.

> CAPTAIN:
> OK. But no tricks!

They approach him nervously. Mitsu studies the sonar.

> TOSUMI:
> Ooooh... a television!

> CAPTAIN:
> (laughing)
> Ha! Crazy kid! This little device tells me when your
> friends the whales are around. It makes killing them so
> much easier!

Mitsu frowns at his delight in saying this.

> CAPTAIN:
> You see, once we see their little green blips on the
> screen, we're on them before they know it! It's called
> "the element of surprise. "Works every time!

> MITSU:
> That's not fair! They don't stand a chance.

> CAPTAIN:
> Fair? Fair? Who ever said anything about this being
> fair? This is a business!

Mitsu is repulsed. The CAPTAIN thrusts his smoke-puffing face into hers.

> CAPTAIN:
> BIG business!

Mitsu backs off the smoke. As she does so, her arm catches a number of maps and charts on the table. They go crashing to the floor! The Captain tries to grab them, loses his balance and crashes over a chair. He is sent sprawling.

CAPTAIN:
Why you... devil kids! Wait till I get my hands on you!

They try to run, first one way, then another. The stumbling Captain cannot catch him. At this moment MITSU notices something on the sonar screen. A swarm of blips!

MITSU:
(whispering to herself)
Toby's pod!

The Captain gives up chasing the elusive Tosumi and returns to the sonar area. Mitsu diverts him by sticking out a foot as he passes her. He falls headlong onto the floor again.

CAPTAIN:
(apoplectic)
Why, you! I'll kill you. Both of you!

The Captain attempts to stand, but as he does so Mitsu pulls his cap down over his eyes. He stumbles around blindly.

CAPTAIN:
Wait till I get my hands on...

Mitsu glances at the sonar. The blips are gone! Mitsu sighs in relief. The Captain goes to grab the kids, but there is suddenly a knock on the door.

CAPTAIN:
(frustrated)
Who is it?

MASAHIRO:
(outside)
Masahiro Kudo, Sir!

CAPTAIN:
(with murder still on his mind)
What do you want?

MASAHIRO:
My children, Sir. It's time for their dinner.

CAPTAIN:
(slowly calming down)
Your children? Your children! Why, you're welcome to them! Come in and get them!

Masahiro enters. He is unaware of what's been going on.

MASAHIRO:

Thank you, Sir. I trust they behaved themselves?

He leads them out of the door. As they exit, Mitsu turns and pokes her tongue out at the Captain. He shakes a fist at her as the unsuspecting Masahiro closes the door in his face.

FADE TO:

BENEATH THE DARK SEA - SAME MOMENT

Murdo leads Toby through dark and inhospitable terrain. They surface for air in the middle of a wide, sticky oil slick. Toby is in a clear spot but Murdo and the gang are caught up in the thick and oily slick. Toby senses that this is a good opportunity to escape. He swims away as hard as he can. Now safe, Toby shelters in a rock cave as a storm brews overhead.

FADE TO:

CABIN ON THE TECHNO SLAYER - EVENING

Mitsu and Tosumi have locked themselves in their cabin. Outside, the storm rages in full fury. The ship is tossed around like a cork. There is an urgent banging on the door.

> MITSU:
> (cautiously)
> Who's there?

> MASAHIRO:
> (outside)
> It's me. Let me in!

Mitsu makes her way to the door and opens it open. MASAHIRO, dripping wet in a yellow slicker, enters.

> MASAHIRO:
> The Captain's sleeping! He didn't tell me what you did,
> but it looks like you've gone too far!

The children snuggle into him apprehensively.

> MITSU:
> (contrite)
> I'm sorry, Father.

> TOSUMI:
> (enthusiastically)
> Me, too!

> MASAHIRO:
> (shaking his head)

What am I going to do with you two?

MITSU:
(her face green, holding her stomach)
You don't think this storm is our punishment, do you?

MASAHIRO:
It's probably nothing compared to what the Captain has in mind for you! Let's hope he just doesn't remember when he does so.

FADE TO:

CAVE AT THE BOTTOM OF THE DARK SEA - NEXT MORNING

The storm is passed. TOBY wakes to hear his name being called.

CHETLY:
Toby! Toby! Where are you?

Toby swims out, delighted to see his old friend.

TOBY:
Chetly! Boy, am I pleased to see you!

CHETLY:
I have good news, dude.

TOBY:
You do?

CHETLY:
Yeah. I found your pod. They sent me to find you!

TOBY:
They did? But I've been banished!

CHETLY:
That's old news. All is forgiven.

TOBY:
Really?

CHETLY:
Yeah. Would I lie to you? (he smiles sweetly) Look, you can either stay here by your lonesome or you can follow me to your pod. The choice is yours.

Toby is delighted to comply.

                              TOBY
              Lead on, Chetly. And be careful, it's dangerous around
              here!

Toby looks around nervously as they swim.

FADE TO:

CABIN ON THE TECHNO SLAYER - LATER THAT DAY

Mitsu's father sits with the children. The storm has passed.

                              MITSU:
              Father? Do you actually like killing whales?

                              MASAHIRO:
              To be honest, Mitsu, I just don't know what I like any
              more. I wish we were all at home with your mother
              right now!

                              MITSU:
              We have caused you much trouble, Father.

                              MASAHIRO:
              Yes, but... I thought I knew so much about life. It all
              seemed so simple. Now I'm wondering.

                              MITSU:
              We all have much to learn from each other.

MASAHIRO smiles. He embraces them with tears in his eyes.

                              MASAHIRO:
              You are such a strange child, Mitsu. Wise and foolish all
              at the same time. I am a very lucky man. I love you both
              so very much!

FADE TO:

BENEATH THE DARK SEA - MORNING

Toby follows Chetly through the outskirts of the Dark Sea. Toby is still looking
around, in fear of the sharks.

                              CHETLY:
              Nearly there!

They swim towards a high coral ridge. Chetly holds back and invites Toby forward.

                              CHETLY:

There, dude. Just over the ridge.

                              TOBY:
          (surprised)
          Aren't you coming?

                              CHETLY:
          (reluctant)
          Er... no. I... er... this is your special moment. Enjoy!

Toby pauses. Chetly appears agitated.

                              CHETLY:
          Go on. They'll be excited to see you!

Toby is excited. He crosses the ridge but finds Murdo and the gang waiting for him.
Toby is immediately surrounded.

                              MURDO:
          Going somewhere... Mister Dreamsinger?

Toby looks betrayed and turns to Chetly.

                              TOBY:
          Why?

Chetly is pathetic in his apology.

                              CHETLY:
          Sorry, Toby. I had to. They said if I didn't do it I'd never
          see The Glow again. I need it, you see. Once you have it
          you can't do without it!

Murdo sneers.

MURDO:
          Yeah, Chetly. "Flow with the Glow", huh! Ha! Ha! Ha!

The gang echoes his derisive laugh. Chetly's eyes drop with the guilt of addiction.

DISSOLVE TO:

BOTTOM OF THE DARK SEA - SAME MOMENT

Diomeda is almost free. He senses something.

                              DIOMEDA:
          (with malevolent relish)
          Ahhhhhhhhh! He is mine! I can smell it!

He devours more toxic slime. With renewed strength he begins to stretch and break the thick viscous threads that hold him.

FADE TO:

OUTSKIRTS OF THE DARK SEA - LATER

Led by his captors, Toby is appalled by the vileness of the accumulated pollution.

                              TOBY:
                    (to himself)
               How could this be?

Toby's is aware of countless mutant sea creatures, all staring at a source of light in the distance - THE GLOW!

CUT TO:

TOBY'S POV - THE GLOW

We see The Glow in all its horrific splendor. Its strange light draws mutant sea creatures like a radiant magnet.

CUT TO:

WIDE SHOT OF THE GLOW - AS BEFORE

Toby too has to fight the impulse to look at it. We now see that it is a sunken, disintegrating nuclear submarine, at the center of which is a green, glowing reactor. Toby scans the unblinking sea creatures for signs of Brujon.

                              TOBY:
               Have you seen my father anywhere, Mr. Murdo?

Murdo pushes him onward.

                              MURDO:
               Who knows? We get all types in here!

A sense of helplessness falls upon Toby and he looks into The Glow's light. Murdo sees this and knocks him away.

                              MURDO:
               What are you trying to do... fry your brain like those sad
               suckers?

Toby notices Chetly staring into the light with the others.

                              TOBY:
               Chetly! My father? Have you seen my father anywhere?

But Chetly remains oblivious. Murdo pushes Toby forward.

> MURDO:
> Move! We have an appointment with the boss!

FADE TO:

BOTTOM OF THE DARK SEA - NEAR DIOMEDA

Toby's body tenses as he hears the thunderous growling of Diomeda. Murdo and the mutant sharks take Toby through the great rock arch that frames the entrance to the vast inner sanctum where Diomeda is. Toby bolts again but Murdo and the gang follow in hot pursuit. They overshoot into the light of The Glow. The sharks become mesmerized, except Murdo, who manages to tear himself away. Then, realizing...

MURDO:
Crap! The boss is gonna kill me!

FADE TO:

BOTTOM OF THE DARK SEA - LATER

Murdo faces the furious Diomeda.

> DIOMEDA:
> Three times you have failed me! But no more! I'll do the
> job myself!

He lashes out at Murdo and sends him headlong into The Glow.

> DIOMEDA:
> Fool!

Diomeda draws every ounce of his strength to pull away from his bonds. Only a few strands of the tenacious oily filth hold him. Suddenly, he stops and sniffs.

> DIOMEDA:
> (sniffing repeatedly)
> Wha..? The singing whale! I can smell him!

He presses his hands to his head in an effort to send out powerful thought waves to Toby.

FADE TO:

CABIN ON BOARD THE TECHNO SLAYER - SAME MOMENT

Mitsu is in the cabin alone. She anxiously stares out of the porthole, scanning the ocean for Toby.

MITSU:
Where are you, Toby? I feel danger. Please beware.

FADE TO:

SOMEWHERE IN THE DARK SEA - SAME MOMENT

Toby cautiously picks his way through the cover of the seabed. Suddenly, he sees Sereena swimming towards Diomeda!

TOBY:
(calling as discreetly as he can)
Sereena! No!

He breaks cover and chases after her.

TOBY:
Sereena! Stop!

Sereena doesn't hear. She reaches the great archway and enters. Toby swims after her but hesitates in the archway.

TOBY:
(filled with fear)
Sereena! Sereena! Come back!

At that moment he hears Sereena scream. His fear dissolves.

TOBY:
Hold on, Sereena. I'm coming!

He swims after her.

DISSOLVE TO:

INNER SANCTUM OF THE DARK SEA - SAME MOMENT

Toby reaches Sereena. She looks frozen and unable to move.

TOBY:
Sereena! What are you doing here?

She looks at him strangely. Then Toby then watches in horror as Sereena transforms into Diomeda! Laughing and leering, the beast whips up the water around Toby.

DIOMEDA:
At last!

Toby is engulfed. Twisting and spinning, he is sucked deeper and deeper into the dark, swirling vortex. It begins to suck the whale helplessly towards Diomeda's hideous wide and gaping mouth as the beast laughs manically!

>   DIOMEDA:
>   Ha! Ha! Ha!

CUT TO:

CABIN ON THE TECHNO SLAYER - SAME MOMENT

Mitsu suddenly grips her throat.

>   MITSU:
>   (screaming)
>   Can't... breathe! Toby! He's suffocating! (then,
>   remembering Thes) Swim with the spirit, Toby! Swim
>   with the spirit! (then) Thes! Help us!

CUT TO:

DIOMEDA'S WHIRLPOOL - SAME MOMENT

Toby is about to be swallowed by Diomeda. But then he hears Mitsu's voice over the tumult of the vortex.

>   MITSU:
>   (echoing v.o.)
>   Swim with the spirit, Toby! Swim with the spirit!

Then Toby hears the voice of Thes joining Mitsu.

>   THES:
>   Swim with the spirit, Toby. The song of the heart has
>   wings!

>   TOBY:
>   (desperately)
>   What?

>   THES:
>   Sing like a Dreamsinger! Sing the song of the Great
>   Mother!

Toby doesn't understand but Mitsu does.

>   MITSU:
>   Toby, open your heart! Sing the sounds of the Great
>   Mother. Like you did before!

Toby gets it. As Diomeda's mouth finally begins to engulf him Toby begins to sing the most beautiful note he has ever sung.

                    TOBY:
              (like a sacred chant)
         Ohhhhhhmmmmmmmmmmmmmmm!

The note is clear, pure and perfect. As Toby sings he begins to glow brightly in the darkness. Diomeda immediately recoils in pain and the whirlpool dissipates. He clutches his chest in pain. Toby is so shocked by the effect that he stops singing. Immediately, Diomeda attacks again.

                    DIOMEDA:
              (more furious than ever)
         Think you're strong, huh? Well, let's see!

Like a fearsome magician Diomeda conjures up a new nightmare. Toby is attacked by enormous black sharks that try to tear his flesh. But Toby begins to sing again.

                    TOBY:
         Ohhhhhhhhhmmmmmmmmmmmmmmm!

Radiant white sharks emerge from the gathering light around him and they rapidly dispatch the black ones. Again, Diomeda recoils.

                    DIOMEDA:
              (struggling for breath)
         Do you really think your pitiful sounds can defeat me,
         whale? You haven't seen anything yet!

Diomeda hurls a barrage of images more terrifying than Toby could ever imagine. Giant black squid tentacles wrap around him and squeeze. Monstrous sea demons, claws slashing, swoop from all sides. Poisonous sea snakes and eels writhe and slither over him, tongues darting, fangs spewing venom. Yet Toby holds strong. From deep within him, a most beautiful sound emerges.

                    TOBY:
              (more powerful than ever)
         Auuuuuuuummmmmmmmmm!

One after another, the demonic creatures are methodically repelled by the light that emanates from Toby. Diomeda's power is failing him. He gorges himself on more toxic waste and with one do-or-die effort he at last breaks himself free from his viscous bondage! An unbelievable transformation takes place. Liberated, Diomeda grows and grows - finally rising above the Dark Sea like an erupting volcano.

CUT TO:

SURFACE OF THE DARK SEA - SAME MOMENT

Turbulence, tidal waves and thunder inflict themselves on everything for miles around. The beast forgets his battle with Toby and laughs madly, mocking at all creation.

> DIOMEDA:
> Ha! Ha! Ha! Now nothing can stand in my way. No
> power on this earth can hold me back!

He seems to increase even further in size and threaten the very heavens. Lightning flashes shower from his head.

CUT TO:

BENEATH THE SURFACE OF THE DARK SEA - SAME MOMENT

Toby realizes he must act fast. He swims to the surface.

CUT TO:

SURFACE OF THE DARK SEA - SAME MOMENT

Toby appears and taunts the towering Diomeda.

> TOBY:
> (at the top of his voice)
> If you're so powerful why did you run away from me?
> Are you scared?

Diomeda looks down on the whale beneath him with contempt.

> DIOMEDA:
> (snorting like a bull)
> Run? From YOU? Huh!

> TOBY:
> (defiantly)
> Yes!

> DIOMEDA:
> You are nothing to me! I could crush you in the palm of
> my hand!

Diomeda's narrowing, reptilian eyes glare menacingly.

> TOBY:
> Yes. But can you stop my song?

Toby goes to sing but Diomeda has other plans. He peers deeply into the Dark Sea. He sees what he's looking for and plucks it from the ocean. He opens his hand and reveals the pale, weak, emaciated figure of Brujon!

                              TOBY:
          Gasp! Father!

Diomeda taunts Toby with Brujon.

                              DIOMEDA:
          This should stop you. Make one sound and I will crush
          him dead!

Toby relents.

                              TOBY:
          No! Don't hurt him. I won't sing!

Diomeda looks smug. But Brujon comes to his senses. Realizing what is going on, he
feebly cries out to Toby.

                              BRUJON:
          Sing, Toby! Sing!

Diomeda scowls and tightens his grip.

                              DIOMEDA:
          Silence, Fool - or you are doomed!

TOBY is torn.

                              TOBY:
          THES! What do I do?

The answer is immediate.

                              THES:
                    (v.o.)
          Surrender your will to the TRUESONG within you. Sing,
          TOBY. Sing like a true Dreamsinger and all will be well.

                              TOBY:
                    (confused)
          But... my father!

                              THES:
          All will be well! Trust me... Dreamsinger!

At that moment, Brujon instinctively rolls himself off Diomeda's hand, tumbling
helplessly towards the surface of the sea far below. He cries out as he does so.

                              BRUJON:
          Sing now, Toby!

Toby sees the flailing body of his father tumbling rapidly towards the sea.

                    TOBY:
        Father! No...!

                    BRUJON:
        (urgently)
        Sing, Toby! Sing!

Toby has to think fast. He reaches deeply into himself and opens his heart. At last he finds his True Voice!

                    TOBY:
            (the song begins weakly at first but it
            soon builds. It is beautiful - quite
            breathtakingly beautiful!)
        Singing

Miraculously, the song breaks Brujon's fall. He floats gently to the water. As if shocked by a searing electrical jolt, Diomeda is in agony. Toby's heart, then his whole body, begins to glow whiter and whiter. The light reaches around Diomeda, who starts to shrink in size. He sinks back through the surface of the Dark Sea and down towards the seabed.

CUT TO:

BENEATH THE DARK SEA - SAME MOMENT

As Toby sings, Diomeda continues to shrink in size and power. The mutant sea creatures in The Glow also change. Their colors return and they become their former selves again. The majesty of Toby's Dreamsong also cleanses and restores the Dark Sea! Diomeda finally shrivels and fades to no more than a dull gray mist. It slithers off to safety.

CUT TO:

AERIAL VIEW OF THE DARK SEA - SHORTLY AFTER

The transformation is wonderful. It is now clean, vibrant and inspirational and even The Glow is no more. The submarine falls into the crack in the ocean bed and its gaping hole is healed and sealed.

CUT TO:

CLOSE-UP OF THE INNER SANCTUM IN THE CORAL REEF - SAME TIME

As Toby's Dreamsong ends, a sacred stillness now fills what was the Dark Sea. All creatures are grateful. Toby even receives unexpected gratitude!

                    MURDO:

(hesitantly)
Mr. Toby?

                    TOBY:

Murdo!

                    MURDO:

I... I want to apologize for all I did. It wasn't me! None of
us! He controlled us!

                    TOBY:
              (with understanding)
Diomeda's power was very strong!

                    MURDO:

              (head bowed)
Indeed it was. I am so very sorry!

Then from behind Toby a familiar voice speaks.

                    BRUJON:

I guess that means you're a Dreamsinger now, eh, Son?

TOBY turns and sees Brujon, now restored.

                    TOBY:

Father! Oh father! I thought you were dead!

They greet each other affectionately. Suddenly, Toby is distracted by a new voice. No
one else hears it.

                    MITSU:

              (v.o.)
Toby! The pod! You must hurry!

Toby looks around, not sure how to respond.

                    BRUJON:

What is it, TOBY?

                    TOBY:

Father, don't ask me how I know this, but mother and
the pod are in great danger!

Toby swims off immediately. Brujon and the others follow.

FADE TO:

DECK OF THE TECHNO SLAYER ~ SAME MOMENT

Mitsu looks out to sea with a shocked expression. Alarms are going off and crew members are rushing to their stations. In the distance Toby's pod is swimming. The ship is slowing, to position itself for the attack.

> MITSU:
> (sending out her thoughts)
> Toby! Hurry! Everyone's in great danger!

DISSOLVE TO:

OPEN SEA - SAME MOMENT

Toby leads the sea creatures towards the pod.

> TOBY:
> Go faster. There's not a moment to lose!

FADE TO:

CABIN ON THE TECHNO SLAYER - SAME MOMENT

Mitsu lies on her bunk and closes her eyes. She begins to "tune in" on Toby, telling Tosumi what's happening.

> MITSU:
> Toby is leading the sea creatures to the pod. They are
> closing in fast.

Tosumi clenches his fist, cheering for Toby and the pod.

> TOSUMI:
> Come on, Toby!

> MITSU:
> Now they can see the pod!

CUT TO:

SMALL CAVE IN THE CORAL REEF - SAME MOMENT

The faded, wisp-like figure of Diomeda is slinking out.

> DIOMEDA:
> So he thinks I'm finished, huh? I'll show him!

He seeks out a single surviving toxic container and consumes its glowing radiation. It makes him stronger. He drifts slowly up to the surface.

CUT TO:

OPEN SEA - SAME MOMENT

Toby, Brujon and the sea creatures swim towards the pod.

> BRUJON
> (calling from behind)
> Can you see them yet, Toby?

> TOBY
> (excitedly)
> Yes. There they are! I can see them!

They accelerate.

FADE TO:

BRIDGE OF THE TECHNO SLAYER - SAME MOMENT

A klaxon blares excitedly. The Captain is chain smoking as usual. The 1ST MATE looks out and then to the instruments.

> 1ST MATE:
> Closing in fast Captain. We'll soon be in range. Strange, though?

> CAPTAIN:
> (through puffs of smoke)
> What?

> 1ST MATE:
> I know this doesn't make sense, but according to sonar there's a huge school of sea creatures heading towards the whales!

The Captain looks at the screen, puzzled and yet delighted.

> CAPTAIN:
> Excellent! Double our kill! This calls for a celebration!

He takes out his hip flask and swigs.

DISSOLVE TO:

AERIAL SHOT OF THE TECHNO SLAYER - SAME MOMENT

The vaporous shadow of Diomeda hovers. He circles, then swoops downward.

CUT TO:

BRIDGE OF THE TECHNO SLAYER - SAME MOMENT

The Captain continues to smoke and drink.

                         CAPTAIN:
          Hee! Hee! Hee! (then, singing) Yo! Ho! Ho! and a bottle
          of rum. Ha! Ha! Ha!

He blows his customary smoke ring and draws the smoke back in as usual. But
Diomeda's mist enters the bridge at that moment and becomes part of the smoke ring.
The Captain sucks him in! Immediately, the Captain's eyes ignite with madness and a
vile smile twists his lips. He cruelly knocks the 1st Mate out and leers at the distant
whales.

                    CAPTAIN/DIOMEDA:
               (guttural, like an animal ready to kill)
          Hah! Hah! Hah!

CUT TO:

SURFACE OF THE OCEAN - SAME MOMENT

Toby leads the sea creatures to the pod. Luma is the first to see Toby. She swims over
and nuzzles him affectionately.

                          LUMA:
          Oh, Toby. I thought we lost you!

Luma looks at him and shakes her head in disbelief.

                          LUMA:
          Look how you've changed! I am so proud of you!

Toby smiles.

                          TOBY:
          I have another surprise for you.

Brujon emerges and Luma is overwhelmed.

                          LUMA:
          Oh, Toby! No!

Luma and Brujon embrace as Sereena approaches.

                          TOBY:
          Sereena!

She is taken aback by his transformation.

                        SEREENA:
          Toby? Is that really you?

Toby just smiles. Now Grampus arrives to see what the fuss is all about. He sees Toby.

                    GRAMPUS:
          What are you doing here? I banished you. Get out of
          here!

                    TOBY:
          The pod is in grave danger. I came to warn you.

                    GRAMPUS:
          Warn me? Who gave you the right to make any
          decisions around here?

Brujon moves forward.

                    BRUJON:
          I did!

Grampus is shocked.

                    GRAMPUS:
          Brujon! But you're...

                    TOBY
          "Dead," Grampus? You don't get rid of me that easily!

Sereena is again frustrated by her father's lack of tact.

                    SEREENA:
          Father, can't you see that everything has changed? For
          once in your life, can you please accept the fact that you
          are wrong!

Grampus looks from Toby to Sereena to Brujon and back. The truth sinks in. He
grumpily swims away to brood alone. Suddenly the mood changes...

                    FEMALE WHALE
               (screaming!)
          Iron Beast!

CUT TO:

BRIDGE OF THE TECHNO SLAYER - SAME MOMENT

The Captain stares through binoculars.

                    CAPTAIN/DIOMEDA:
               (madly)
          Faster! Faster!! Faster!!!

CUT TO:

CABIN ON THE TECHNO SLAYER - SAME MOMENT

Mitsu is still with Tosumi. Suddenly she is shocked.

                    MITSU:
          (frantic)
     Oh, no!

She rushes out with Tosumi following in hot pursuit.

                    MITSU
     Quick!

CUT TO:

SURFACE OF THE OCEAN - SAME MOMENT

The pod is in panic mode and instinctively turns to Brujon.

                    1ST HUMPBACK:
     BRUJON, what do we do?
                    2ND HUMPBACK:
          (nervous)
     Help us! The entire pod awaits Brujon's instructions but
     Brujon turns to his son.

                    BRUJON:
     Toby?

Toby is surprised as the pod turns to him. He thinks quickly.

                    TOBY:
     Quick! Behind me! We'll face them!

The pod is suddenly agitated.

                    3RD WHALE:
     Face them?

                    4TH WHALE:
     No! We cannot! The Iron Beast will destroy us!

                    TOBY:
     No, it won't. Not if we all join together! Trust me!

But there is still a sense of rebellion.

                    1ST WHALE:

No! It's madness!

                    3RD WHALE:
We'll be slaughtered!

                    2ND WHALE:
Brujon, speak to your son. He is crazy. He asks too
much!

Brujon ignores them. He proudly maneuvers behind Toby.

                    BRUJON:
Toby, I am with you.

The pod is in total disarray - then Grampus steps in!

                    GRAMPUS:
              (somewhat grudgingly)
Brujon is right. Toby knows more than all of us! I am
with him, too!

Grampus moves beside Brujon. Members of the pod look amazed. Sereena is grateful
to her father and joins him, too. The others are now convinced. They all stand behind
Toby, one by one.

                    TOBY:
              (to all)
It WILL take courage. But we can do it!

                    BRUJON:
Toby is right. We must run and hide no longer!

                    GRAMPUS:
Yes! (then, to Toby) We... I... am sorry!

It is a magnificent sight. Hundreds of whales and other sea creatures line up behind
Toby.

CUT TO:

BRIDGE OF THE TECHNO SLAYER - SAME MOMENT

The CAPTAIN/DIOMEDA sees Toby. His eyes narrow malevolently.

                    CAPTAIN/DIOMEDA:
              (leering and hissing)
Still the brave whale, eh?

He shuts the ship's engine down to HALT.

CUT TO:

SURFACE OF THE OCEAN - SAME MOMENT

An ominous silence hangs over everything. All that can be heard is the movement of the sea and the crying of gulls. The amplified CAPTAIN/DIOMEDA's voice resounds.

> CAPTAIN/DIOMEDA:
> (to the crew)
> Kill that whale in front! He is their leader. (then, to
> Toby) The time has come to die, Dreamsinger. You will
> not escape me this time!

TOBY recognizes the voice.

> TOBY:
> Diomeda!

CUT TO:

DECK OF THE TECHNO SLAYE' - SAME MOMENT

MASAHIRO loads his gun and prepares to fire. He aims.

CUT TO:

TOBY AND SEA CREATURES - AS BEFORE

A strange sound begins to echo across the waters as Toby begins his Dreamsong. A beautiful colored light emanates from him and spirals up to a column of shimmering light that eventually surrounds all the sea creatures.

> TOBY:
> (singing)
> Singing his Dreamsong.

CUT TO:

WIDER VISION OF THE OCEAN - SAME MOMENT

The wildness of the waves is stilled by Toby's song. Even the gulls are silent! The column of iridescent light parts the clouds and sunlight streams through on the splendor of the scene. Now other sea creatures join in the song too.

> TOBY/SEACREATURES/POD:
> All singing Toby's Dreamsong.

CUT TO:

DECK OF THE TECHNO SLAYER - AS PREVIOUS SHOT

The crew are captivated and transformed by the beauty of the song. They stop what they are doing and listen. Only Masahiro remains obediently at his post. The Captain/Diomeda winces in great pain as the Dreamsong unfolds but screams to Masahiro.

CAPTAIN/DIOMEDA:
Fire! Now, you fool! Fire!

Masahiro lines up the sights, then hesitates.

CAPTAIN/DIOMEDA:
Masahiro - kill that whale!

Mitsu and Tosumi burst forward. Mitsu screams to her father.

MITSU:
Father! NO!

She runs up and grabs his arm and tugs at it.

MITSU:
Father, please don't. Toby saved Tosumi's life!
Remember? Listen to him. Listen to his song.

Meanwhile the pain of Captain/Diomeda becomes overbearing.

CAPTAIN/DIOMEDA:
No! Don't listen! Shut your ears! KILL THAT WHALE!

But Masahiro too is entranced by the beauty of the Dreamsong. He lets go of the harpoon, defiantly.

CUT TO:

BRIDGE ON THE TECHNO SLAYER - SAME MOMENT

The CAPTAIN/DIOMEDA clasps his hands to his ears.

CAPTAIN/DIOMEDA:
Arrrrrh! I can't stand it! (then, staggering) I have to...
kill...that whale!

He staggers from the bridge and scrambles down to the lower deck. Crewmen attempt to block his path but, crazed, he knocks them over like tenpins. He seizes the harpoon, aims it and pulls the trigger!

MITSU:
Scream!

CUT TO:

SURFACE OF THE OCEAN - SAME TIME

The harpoon arcs in slow motion towards Toby. The CAPTAIN/DIOMEDA jumps and yells in triumphant anticipation. Stunned, every sea creature stops singing - except Toby. But the harpoon is deflected by the column of light that surrounds them all. It drops harmlessly into the sea.

CUT TO:

DECK OF THE TECHNO SLAYER - SAME TIME

The CAPTAIN/DIOMEDA watches with blinking, incoherent disbelief. He is an emotional wreck.

                    CAPTAIN/DIOMEDA:
          (muttering madly)
          I... I cannot let him... beat me! I... must destroy... that
          whale! I must!

Filled with a fury that goes beyond reason he launches himself overboard. He thrashes at the water but his inebriation and fury mean he can't swim. He begins to drown. The possessing spirit of Diomeda deserts the Captain's flailing body. Its wispy, phantom-like form rises-up above the ship, muttering and cursing.

                    DIOMEDA:
          You will never finish me! I will feed off this world's
          greed and your ignorance - and become strong again!
          My power will always remain to haunt you! Ha! Ha! Ha!
          He becomes a twisting vortex and is carried away by the
          wind.

CUT TO:

SURFACE OF THE SEA - SAME MOMENT

The Captain struggles in the water. He is almost drowned.

                    CAPTAIN:
          Help me! (Gurgle) Save me!

Masahiro rows a lifeboat to them and Mitsu reaches out for the drowning Captain. But they cannot quite reach him. At this moment Chetly appears and nudges the Captain towards the children. He is saved.

                    MURDO:
          (with renewed respect)
          And I always thought you were a loser! How wrong can
          you be!

Chetly grins.

CHETLY:
Hey, dude. Never doubt the dolphin!

The lifeboat drifts towards Toby and the other sea creatures.

CUT TO:

HEAD-ON MEDIUM SHOT - MITSU IN THE BOAT

Mitsu is excited as the boat draws near.

CUT TO:

WIDE SHOT OF THE OPEN SEA - PROFILE SHOT

The boat halts. Mitsu smiles. Toby smiles. She instinctively leans out and throws her arms around the young whale. Then she gives him a huge kiss on the end of his nose!

MITSU:
I love you, Toby whale!

Suddenly the mood of the moment is broken by a scurrying in the water around one of the boat's oars. A flurry of splashing reveals Toby's old friend, Crusty!

CRUSTY:
(trying to steady himself)
Oooooh! Errrrp! Arrrrrgh! (then, steady!) Heard your
Dreamsong Toby. Great set of pipes you have there,
man! Saw the colors too. Wow, cool colors! Ooooops!

He loses his balance and splashes into the water again!

SFX
Plop!

They all laugh as the camera starts a very long, slow pullback on the whole scene.

THES:
(v.o.)
And so it was that a young whale faced his greatest fear
and became the Dreamsinger that fulfilled a legend.
(pause) But that is just the beginning of the tale!

LONG FADE OUT:

THE END - TITLE CREDITS

During the credit sequence we see Toby and Sereena swimming joyfully with their young children. They enter a familiar cave and introduce them to the aging Maestro Baleeni who gives them singing lessons!